No. 41 Burlington Road

Jack C. Phillips

Camelot Publishing Company

No. 41 Burlington Road
Copyright © 2014 by Jack C. Phillips
All rights reserved. Printed in the United Kingdom.
No part of this book may be used or reproduced
in any manner whatsoever without written permission
except in the case of brief quotations embodied in
critical articles and reviews.

For my beautiful girls Molly, Ludmila, Natália & Shannon.

And for Neide Rocha for all your hard work and endeavours.

Acknowledgement

I would like to thank all at Camelot for their inspiration, particularly Editor and head honcho Mica Rossi for her help, her patience, and most of all, for her belief.

To my very good friend Billy
Thank you for - well just
for being
Jack Phillips

Foreword

My relationship with Jack C. Phillips began in August of 2013, when I received an online invitation to join an elite group of artists and authors to participate in an exclusive project. It was a seductive invitation and guaranteed to make a person want to stay around and see what the next day might bring.

What the next day brought was this - Jack took a group of very dissimilar writers and somehow knit us into a cohesive group of authors. We soon learned, under his tutelage, to play off each others' words. From the simplest of suggestions, he showed us how to spark wondrous and improbable ideas and make them believable. He hounded us, railed at us, and pushed us to our limits. Some fell by the wayside when they couldn't keep up. Some were killed off with no chance of redemption. The rest of us lived and loved, died and were reborn, and steadily became better writers. Including Jack.

Like all good things, that initial group came to several very fiery ends, but we have carried on in one form or another since. Through each incarnation, Jack has been the harper plucking our strings, throwing plot twists at us that have made us groan but have made us think, a master spider weaving the complicated webs we've traveled. And travel them gladly we have.

What does all this have to do with No. 41 Burlington Road? Nothing. And everything. There may be others out there who could have taken the same group of inexperienced writers and turned them into a functioning team. Who might even have contributed to the group's ongoing storylines with wit and dedication. But not all of them could have penned a novel like Burlington Road.

Because Burlington Road is Phillips at his purest and most intense, spinning his own webs for the children of his mind to follow. And it's *good*. Rich in characters and rife with secrets, No. 41 Burlington Road takes the reader on a journey through a typical suburban neighborhood and rips the mask off to expose its nerves.

But as with any other novel, there is more to a compelling read than the characters, no matter how well-fleshed they are, and Phillips does not disappoint. His unmistakably British style, rather than detracting from the story, lends it a certain charm that balances its darker elements and keeps you reading from chapter to chapter far into the night. The author has a knack for turning a phrase that more than once plunged me into the thick of the story and then brought me back later to savor that line again long after I had finally closed the covers of the book.

But more than that, Phillips makes you genuinely care about what happens to the inhabitants of his fictitious neighborhood, and that, to me at least, is what makes a satisfying story.

I could go on, but rather than spoil your fun, I'll let you discover for yourself the magic of No. 41 Burlington Road. Turn the page, open the door, walk into the parlour…

Mica Rossi

March 2014

Prologue

Caring, I found, was the hardest part.

It was really difficult to get an interest in things when you felt so disconnected. It was almost like accepting you were dying. Like you were letting go bit by bit. The depression had lifted, thankfully and the sadness had faded; still there, but muted like the buzz of an insect when you cover it over with a jar.

It lived with me like an old friend, and I found everything tinged with it. The birth of a baby, destined to die. Familiar places that stood frozen in time, a testament to endurance, when everything that made them special and familiar had long since gone.

Time itself was the saddest concept, like it had caught up with its own tomorrow and had nowhere else to go.

'Of time you would make a stream, upon whose banks you would sit and watch its flowing.'

I sat that day by my own personal time stream and saw it was barren and without life, its banks yellow and parched, its riverbed cracked and dry.

I didn't mind though. I shrugged and moved on, because caring, I found, was becoming increasingly difficult.

Chapter One

I never went out again after she left. I became a prisoner in my own home. Under house arrest and shackled by my own restraints, I lived a virtual existence which consisted mainly of internet shopping, black and white films and watching the world go by.

Life beyond my door became a soap opera. Something unknown, something to be feared, and fear itself became both my gaoler and my sanctum.

My prison? A bland, ordinary house, on a dull everyday street, in a boring run-of-the-mill town. Burlington Road was built in the nineteen thirties, and apart from the two end houses that were doodle-bugged in forty-four, it survived the war relatively unscathed.

Every house had the same bone structure. A solid but basic thirties design with touches of deco. Obviously there were one or two modern additions, car ports, faux bay windows, storm porches, etc. Our house though, had no such additions. My wife, my soon-to-be *ex*-wife, had a passion for all things thirties and embraced its original features rather than trying to cover them up.

The street itself was in a typical, middle-class suburban area; it was a wide road framed with grass verges and the occasional poplar. Its layout basically consisted of one detached house neighbouring a semi, neighbouring another detached house and so on until the end of the road. It was the same on both sides of the street, and I lived in one of the semis, number forty-one right in the middle, giving me an unrestricted view over most of the street and free reign to speculate over the comings and goings of my neighbours. It's strange how other people's lives take on a new significance when your own was on a back-burner.

I was a writer, of sorts. I wrote jingles and ad campaigns for a local radio station. So it stood to reason that I was a people watcher. I observed and made notes. A voyeur if you like, of mankind and all of its eccentricities and someone equally blessed and cursed with an overly-vivid imagination.

Last night, for instance I dreamed I was in a big house. I knew it was mine, but it wasn't the place I was living in then. The house had four floors and lots of rooms. The fourth floor was a mystery to me. It was dark, dreary and unused and in my dream I had decided to utilise it, to open it up. I came across a door that had been blocked off in the back of a cupboard and went in to investigate. I found a staircase and had barely climbed three steps when I was overcome by the sensation of being watched and such a feeling of evil around me that I turned and ran.

The dream directory told me that the house represented me, my mind, and that the fourth floor was part of my psyche, a part of me that I was afraid of and kept locked away, which when I came to think about it, was actually not far from the truth.

Life was surreal in my little bubble. Time had no significance there. Minutes seemed like hours and hours dragged on for days. My phone had long been disconnected and my letters remained unopened.

I sent text messages to various family members, informing them that I was fine, but needed time alone. So apart from the occasional email from work, the only people I saw then were the man who delivered my groceries, the postman and my neighbours.

The residents of Burlington Road were a fairly mixed bag. Some had lived here for years, like my immediate neighbours at number thirty-nine, Jeremy and Margaret. (Or Victor and Margaret Meldrew as my ex used to call them.) Graham at forty-two, Alan at forty-three and the old dear Clara across at number thirty-eight.

My neighbours were creatures of habit, Victor trimming his hedges every third Sunday of the month, weather permitting and Margaret walking the dogs promptly at eight every morning, whatever the weather. They took regular trips in their caravan, belonged to various clubs and associations and had a fetish for Yorkshire Terriers. Pretension aside, Victor and Margaret were a fairly ordinary couple.

Clara left for bingo on Wednesday afternoons and caught the bus into town every Tuesday to go shopping. She was a colourful character, but had really started slowing down recently. In fact, I hadn't seen her for a couple of days and I wondered had my life still been in full swing, would I have cared? Would I have even noticed?

Chapter 2

Clara

Clara sighed as she knocked dust off the old radio, sneezing as the disturbed particles formed a cloud that settled in her hair and on her shoulders. Catching a glimpse of herself in the mirror above the mantle, she noticed the dark rings and deep lines etched into her skin beating a path from the corner of her eyes. The grey roots of her hair, a stark contrast to the brassy auburn tips. A well managed coiffure, belying the sparseness of her scalp.

She sat back heavily in her moth-eaten armchair. One arthritic hand curled around the armrest while the other fingered an old silver locket she wore. She sat motionless for a while, her eyes misting over as distant memories played on in her mind, like scenes from an old movie reel.

No-one visited her much anymore. Her one and only son had moved away with her grandchildren. He hardly even phoned these days.

She thought of her own grandmother and how she always had a clean lace handkerchief and smelled of lavender. She brushed away a tear before it could roll down her cheek.

'I think I have a tissue somewhere,' she remarked to no-one in particular.

Reaching for her bag from a small table beside her chair, Clara's hand brushed a withered poinsettia that sat half dead and dejected in its pot; a large brown leaf detached itself and fell silently to its final resting place on the floor.

'Oh dear.' Her voice sounded vacant in the large but sparsely furnished room.

She struggled awhile with the clasp of her handbag before grabbing a tissue, and with trembling hands she wiped away a tear that had long since dried.

Chapter Three

I was browsing the internet, seeking inspiration for a radio advert for a firm of local solicitors. Outside, the wind beat the rain with ferocity against the window pane, where it rolled its way south in an ever increasing stream of submission.

It was well after two in the afternoon and we'd barely seen light all day. I didn't mind! Unlike my neighbour, Graham at number forty-two, I liked days like this. Seeing the sun shining somehow made me feel restless and guilty for wasting my days indoors on the computer. The truth was, I couldn't go out even if I'd wanted to.

I got distracted by Facebook and ended up joining causes I cared little about, signing petitions and deliberately avoiding the increasing amount of messages from friends, invites to events, birthday requests and offers to join this person or that in a game of something or other.

A friend of a friend was complaining about the growing number of unemployed youth, and someone's cousin had posted her wedding album for all to see. The bride and groom stared apathetically at the camera, the page boy was scowling and the best man's hand was on the bride's arse.

I looked, via the page of someone's brother I'd met once at a party, at the page of someone I knew vaguely years ago and then wished I hadn't. Amid the requiems and pictures of her beloved departed and under the guise of wall postings, she spun a sorry tale of a tragic life. She was alone, under forty, had seven kids and was divorced from an abusive spouse. The worst thing was she, like everyone else on Facebook, had hundreds of 'friends' from her past, and none of them knew these things about her because no-one bothered to ask.

I decided to deactivate my page. Facebook should have been called façade book, or better, false façade book! I flipped back to my home page and found myself staring mindlessly at news flashes and snippets of celebrity gossip.

Suddenly I heard a car pull up and found the hushed purring of its engine vaguely comforting. I knew instantly who it was; Graham at forty-two, back from the office. I watched him for a while and smiled to myself as he got out, kicking the door shut and balancing his briefcase on his head, cursing the weather as usual. Inasmuch as I didn't like the man, I found the familiarity of his daily routine reassuring.

Overhead the dark clouds came together, a silent conspiracy of weightless nebula shutting out any remainder of blue. A beautiful, but somehow menacing sight.

In the gloom of my office, illuminated only by my computer screen, I sat down and began to write.

Chapter Four

Graham

Graham kicked off his shoes and returned his rain-sodden coat to its hook. The water from his hair ran in streams down the back of his neck, and his spectacles misted in the overly heated hallway.

'Is that you Graham?' his mother called out from her makeshift bedroom in the lounge.
He cursed silently, after a hard day at the office filing tax returns and counting other people's money. Seeing how the other half live and achieve and profit, he had to come home to that nagging, crippled old hag.

'One day,' he hissed under his breath. 'One day.'

His mind wandered to the pretty blonde girl in the basement. So young, he mused. So tender. His rubbery lips glistened and his eyes glinted behind his glasses.

'Spirited young thing.' He leered. 'Put up quite a fight.'

'Graham!' His mother's sharp tone brought him abruptly back to the present. 'Mummy needs the toilet.'

He caught his reflection again in the hallway mirror.

'Soon,' he promised himself.

Chapter Five

I spent another night spent lost in a Prozac haze, drifting in and out of consciousness. My mind was foggy, my dreams lurid and frighteningly real. Around two, I was roused by the sound of a baby crying. I got out of bed, tripping over Bogart the cat on my way to toilet. He hissed at me.

'Charming,' I said, rubbing my blurry eyes and trying hard to focus.

The noise that disturbed me had stopped, but I heard sounds from the street and went over to the window to investigate. Directly across from me was number forty, a rental house that had lain empty for a good few years.

It stood with a brooding, vacant air and I wondered why no-one ever stayed there for very long. According to Clara, its immediate neighbour, it had always been so and was a cold, damp and unloved house. Its owner was an old guy who had been in a care home for many years.

A sudden movement among the shadows in next door's driveway caught my attention. Graham was outside in his pyjamas and he was putting something into his garage. Something in a large, green rubble sack. I looked over at my alarm clock. Twenty to four. What the hell was he doing at this time of night?

Graham had lived on the street longer than I could remember. His elderly mother, crippled I think, was housebound. He was a strange man. He always seemed angry, but when confronted he backed down to a simpering, obsequious weasel of a man.

My ex, Beth, had torn a strip off him more than once, when Graham had locked Bogart in his garage during a spate of animal disappearances from the neighbourhood.

He reminded me of Mr. Harvey in 'The Lovely Bones.' It was weird a man of his age having no friends or girlfriends. Living with his mother and never socialising or going out. It never occurred to me to wonder what people thought of *me*.

It seemed I had just dropped off again when the removal van woke me up from a dream. I had gone down to the kitchen to feed Bogart and seen another cat at his bowl. The cat was huge and grey, a tabby I think, but it had perfectly even stripes, like Spot in the Hong Kong Phooey cartoon, and I suddenly felt curiously afraid. I tried to shoo it out, but it wouldn't budge. I opened the French doors and grabbed the brush. I didn't want to hurt the beast, but he filled me with a strange feeling of dread.

There was something very wrong about this cat and besides, I didn't want him attacking Bogart, who I could hear clawing at the kitchen door.

After a few circles around the central island in the kitchen with me in hot pursuit, the cat turned to me with a look of contempt and calmly walked out. I quickly shut the door behind it, but instead of walking away, it just sat looking at me as if waiting to be let back in.

Bogart, who had managed to put a paw through a crack in the kitchen door and let himself in, completely ignored the cat and went to his food. It was as though he didn't know it was there at all. When he'd finished, he sat at the door facing the monster cat and waiting to be let out. I looked up at the cat and saw it had the biggest, bluest eyes I had ever seen. Then the cat grinned at me and in its mouth I saw a perfect set of human teeth.

I awoke abruptly in a cold sweat. I couldn't understand why the dream had been so creepy, or why I had been so afraid of a cat!

A chink of light filtered its way through the crack I had left in the curtains, when I was watching Graham. Bogart had made himself comfortable again and gave a gentle snore from the foot of the bed. I tapped him playfully with my toe. Prozac dreams, I wondered, or the occasional recreational drug I'd shared with my friend Joaquin coming back to haunt me?

At the thought of Joaquin, I was overcome with a sudden feeling of loss. I knew the removal van was going to his house, number thirty-seven, or rather, the house he gave away when rumour had it he left to live on a Tibetan mountain and become a Shaolin monk.

Joaquin, the perpetual drifter. He was always moving around, travelling the world. His life was one big adventure. Half Irish, half Brazilian, his parents had died in a car crash when he was young, leaving him with the house (less a mortgage) and a substantial amount in life assurance, most of which he'd gifted to various charities. He lived a modest, simple life and worked for the most part overseas as a volunteer for one cause or another.

And he was quite a character! We'd get up one day and find him sitting in the kitchen, drinking Beth's camomile tea, just back from working in some Peruvian emerald mine or somewhere equally bizarre.

We never knew, nor did we ask, how he'd got in; probably the same way as the cat in my dream. But this time I had a horrible feeling that I would never see him again, and I couldn't have imagined the terrible vacuum this would create in my life.

Chapter Six

Joaquin

In getting to know Joaquin better, I discovered what a complex character he was, the likes of which I'd never known before. Benevolent, kind, heroic even. He'd once fought off six lads who were trying to steal an old lady's handbag, never once patting himself on the back or bragging about it. On the contrary, Joaquin had vowed me to secrecy, upset at having hurt a couple of the lads in the scuffle (it going against his pacifist's doctrine) and in telling my pals the tale, I'd succeeded only in pissing him off somewhat and increasing his army of admirers even more.

Tall and broad shouldered with even features, twinkling blue eyes and a mop of unruly curls, Joaquin could have resembled an old boot and people would still have loved him. I could only watch as he befriended friends of friends on Facebook, convincing them first of all that they had met before, charming and seducing his way in their hearts and minds with no intentions of ever meeting up.

Joaquin exuded an inner power and he knew it. Women, Beth included, both married and single, fell head over heels in love with him and flirted shamelessly. Men bonded instantly, soon believing they'd known him all their lives, offering him with very little encouragement a pint, a bed for the night, eternal friendship and undying loyalty.

Alan, my neighbour at forty-three, adored him, and what I knew was a platonic friendship for Joaquin, I suspected had a whole different meaning for Alan.

He was frighteningly intelligent and worldly, and as a Buddhist he seemed to exert control not only over his own mind, but also the minds of others. His kind words and wisdom, both genuine and heartfelt, won him as many admirers as his sickeningly handsome features. No demon this! People's lives were enriched and improved on meeting Joaquin.

From his distant, impenetrable world, like a virtual messiah he mended many broken hearts, healed the mentally and physically sick, reunited estranged families and stopped many a divorce, although having probably been the unwitting cause of many of them in the first place.

Beth and I first met Joaquin when we moved to Burlington Road about five years ago and instantly bonded with him. In all that time, I had never known him to be in one place for longer than six months at a time. He found jobs on tug boats and cargo ships, often working for his fare to far-flung destinations. He picked grapes in California, worked with homeless children in Rio and taught English in Hong Kong. He spoke several languages fluently and was knowledgeable about cultures and civilisations all over the world.

It was kind of sad then to think of him sitting alone in some grotty B&B opposite the dock, awaiting his fare, having long since given away his house and possessions to some charitable cause or other. Never still, never resting, never settling or belonging anywhere, and later as he lay on his berth in his cabin staring at the ceiling, I wondered what he'd be thinking and where his meditation would lead him.

In my mind's eye, I saw him, Joaquin Fitzpatrick, eternal nomad, bundling his few possessions together on hearing the ship's horn and making his way through the silent mist towards the docks and the waiting vessel. As he walks along the ill-lit quay, his shadow mingles with the shadows of other wandering souls and is soon lost to the enveloping darkness.

Chapter Seven

A family moved into number thirty-seven. A thirty-something couple and their son. I couldn't help but pick up on the woman's perfectly rounded vowels as she called after the little terror who ran from the car and tore around the front gardens, flattening or uprooting anything and everything in his path.

There's something not quite right about a family with a new BMW, Armani suits and a son called Tristan moving into a modest semi in Pleasantville. A semi, I happen to know, they picked up for a song.

I watched as the removal men carried out their furniture. Nothing special there, all modern, all modest, and I'm sure I saw a couple of Ikea boxes in amongst the regular furniture.

The guy, a proper Quentin, slammed the car door and rushed into the house, leaving his wife to chase after the boy and supervise the move. I studied her for a moment, then she turned suddenly and looked up at my window, almost as if she had sensed someone was there. I reddened and moved away, embarrassed at being caught out, but not before I'd noticed the bruising, scarcely hidden behind those Gucci sunglasses.

Chapter Eight

Graham

The rain stopped as Graham pulled into the lay-by. He removed his glasses, rubbing his tired eyes.

He mumbled angrily under his breath, bringing the flat of his hand down heavily on the steering wheel. It wasn't fair. Why him? He'd heard rumours of redundancies at his workplace and knew instinctively, unpopular as he was, that he would be first in the firing line.

Those bastards at the office, whispering about him and giggling with those tarts from Personnel. Laughing at him, ridiculing him! Twenty-seven years he had served with Barton, Withnall and Reeve as a clerk and somehow, he had always been overlooked when it came to promotion. Overlooked for someone younger, someone smarter…fitter!

He got out of the car, slamming the door in his customary heavy-handed manner. It sounded unusually loud in the peaceful surroundings, but he knew that nobody would hear it this deep into the woods.

The night was calm. No whisper of the wind through the trees. Not even the cracking of twigs as night creatures stirred in the undergrowth. The moon lay hidden behind a large bank of cloud, but that suited Graham's purpose well. Besides he always kept a torch in the car.

His face grew dark in the dim stillness of the night, and angry thoughts taunted him as he opened the car boot, taking from it a large green sack, which he slung over his shoulder.

He thought about the women from work, 'hussies' his mother had called them, flaunting themselves in front of him, teasing him in their tight pencil skirts and low-cut tops…well he'd show them. He'd show them all.

He made his way through the trees and his feet quickly became soaked in the sodden undergrowth. The beam of his torch was faint, a conspiracy of overhead branches filtering out any natural light.

Once or twice he stumbled over a fallen branch or a root, having at one point to reach out to a nearby tree to stop himself from falling, almost dropping the sack he carried. He hugged the trunk for a moment while he caught his breath, enjoying the fresh woodland scent and the feeling of bark, rough against his skin. He set off again, slowly this time, checking for roots and other trip hazards with his torch.

He thought again of work and scowled. Treating me like dirt, he mused. After all those years of service. Well, he'd make them pay, those rotten bastards…somehow!

He stopped when he reached the disused quarry deep in the woods and dumped the heavy sack, rolling it with his foot until it rested perilously on the edge of the drop. With one almighty kick, he sent his cargo crashing into the pit. Panting and red faced with exertion, he sat down heavily on the ground and reaching for his handkerchief, he patted his face and neck, now bathed in perspiration.

Around him the woods kept a silent vigil, solemn and respectful of the ceremony he had just performed, only a dull thud breaking the peaceful repose of the night. Graham grinned as he imagined hearing the cracking of bones as the sack hit the quarry floor.

Chapter Nine

I dreamt I was invited to a party on the top floor of a skyscraper. It was an executive party, and I was panicking as I was already running late. When I finally arrived at the venue, there was a queue of people standing out front, so I tried to find another way in.

The fire exit at the back of the building was ajar, so I made my way through and managed to find the lifts. The illuminated display of one of the lifts indicated it was on the ground floor and I opened the doors without hesitating and stepped in, but there was no lift there, just a terrifying, dark void and a shaft that seemed to drop into the very depths of hell.

I sat up with a jolt, suddenly wide awake. My head was fuzzy and wouldn't clear and it seemed like forever before I was able to drop off again. It was at times like that when I missed human company the most. I ran my hand across Beth's cold, empty pillow and turned my head towards the window. I caught a glimpse of dawn's sombre light, breaking its way through the inky, night sky before falling into a restless, haunted sleep.

Day after day, I watched as the leaves of the oak, at the bottom of the garden, turned first red and then yellow, before finally being detached and dropping to the ground.

The days were drawing in, the nights were colder and still I hadn't ventured out. I desperately needed to go out back and saw up some logs. The house would be freezing soon if I didn't. I had to pull myself together. Beth wasn't coming back, I knew that and I couldn't stay cooped up in the house forever.

I needed my life back. I *wanted* my life back, but every time I tried to step out, I would be overcome by such fear the likes of which I had never experienced before. The vista would swim before me, wildly distorted. Sometimes widening, sometimes narrowing to a tube. Just a circle of world surrounded by nothingness, and I feared that if I stepped out, I would lose the path and be sucked into the void. I would become dizzy and breathless with fear and only when I shut my eyes tightly and stepped back inside, would my breathing slow, my heartbeat regulate and the world around me stop spinning.

I knew I had to start communicating again. I couldn't shut people out permanently. So far, my family and friends had abided by my wish for privacy, but they wouldn't stay away forever, nor did I want them to.

I had resolved to plug the phone back in; maybe that was the first logical step towards getting back into the swing of things. I stared dumbly at the instrument while its display lit up and it reset itself with a beep.

Without warning, it sprang to life and I all but jumped out of my skin. I just couldn't move. My hands were sweating and I was shaking like a leaf. I reached out nervously to pick it up, my fingers hovering over the receiver like the claws of a hawk waiting to swoop. The ringing reverberated around the room, unusually loud, and it grated on my nerves. I suddenly leapt forward and pulled the cable from the wall. The silence was abrupt and almost as deafening as the ringing. With my face buried in my hands, I sank to the floor and wept.

It seemed like hours had passed before I finally moved. I must have slept, because I remember nothing of it, except a concerned tomcat rubbing against my jeans. I tried to get up but my legs had turned to jelly. So I pulled myself up with the arm of the sofa and stood there unsteadily until the feeling returned and I was able to walk.

That was the first time, the only time I would ever cry for Beth!

Ours was never a match made in heaven, but we loved each other once. Beth was beautiful, clever and extremely popular. I was moody, shy and insecure. While she was fiercely ambitious, not just for herself but also for me, I was calm, laid-back and content to plod along. I worked to live, she lived to work. I always knew she'd get fed-up and leave one day. She said tom-*ah*-to, I said tom-*ay*-to, she called the whole thing off, leaving me with the cat, the house and surprisingly few regrets.

I decided to open my mail, which would be a start, and then maybe turn my mobile on in silent mode. If I couldn't handle talking to people just yet, at least they could send me messages. The letters were mostly junk as I suspected. Over-fifties life insurance plans and offers of buy one, get one free at the local supermarkets. A few bills covered by direct debit, so no worries there. Bank statements, accountant's letters and several official looking missives all from the same place. I recognised the name franked on the envelope. It was Beth's solicitor.

After filing all but the bank statements in the bin, I suddenly felt better and decided I was going to do something with the house. If it was to be my prison, then at least it would be comfortable, and I hadn't really done much in the way of tidying since she left.

I found several tea chests in the loft from when we bought the house and began collecting the few things she'd left behind, including any wedding photos and her pillow, which still smelled vaguely of her scent. There were also things she'd bought for our home, cushions, prints, ornaments and the like.

When I'd neutralised the house, I put everything into the chests in the spare room, the smallest room having pretensions of being my office even though I did most of my work on the dining room table. When I'd finished, I felt as though I had cleared some of the fog from my mind. I threw myself down on the sofa, much to Bogart's annoyance, and treated myself to a beer.

A sudden, insane resolve to saw those logs hit me and I strode confidently to the French doors and threw them open. I stepped out cautiously and then the world started to spin. My heart began to race alarmingly and I stepped back as quickly as my condition would allow and closed the doors.

Two beers later and I had devised a plan. The logs were piled up right outside the door, and my saw was stored with my other tools, in the little room at the back of the house that had originally been the larder. I would lie on the floor, close my eyes, drag the logs indoors and cut them up right there on the dining room floor.

The cat fled as soon as the circular saw began screaming. There was sawdust all over the place, but I loved it. When I'd sawed through most of the pile and had enough firewood to see me through the whole of winter and well into spring, I stopped.

The sawdust was everywhere, but I managed to hoover most of it up. It was then I noted, with some satisfaction, the damage the dirty logs and sawdust had done to Beth's new cream Berber. Heading towards the kitchen for another celebratory beer, I took off my wedding ring and dropped it down the waste disposal.

And that's when the disturbances began…

Chapter Ten

Joaquin

Joaquin stood alone on deck looking out to sea.

Behind him the quay, shrouded in mist, was reduced to a string of flickering lights like the Christmas tree lights of a dim and distant past.

His heart yearned for no-one, nor did he feel remotely lonely. From below deck he could hear the raucous laughter of the lads settling in to their new ship, enjoying a beer or two and a game of cards on their first night aboard. Soon he would join them, but first he wanted some quiet time, some time for reflection, as he watched the sun sink into a line of fire on the horizon.

Where he was going was a mystery even to him. Where he ended up he didn't care. For all the tales of Tibetan mountains circulating back home, he had no destination in mind. He had spent some time in York and then Dublin with distant relations, and then taken a job last minute working in the engine room of a cargo ship bound for North Africa. He thought maybe he'd jump ship at Tunisia and take in Morocco and possibly Mauritania before making further plans.

In three or four days they would arrive in Rome, where he would spend his first day of leave visiting a city he knew and loved well. Normally he would jump at the chance of visiting the Galleria Nazionale D'Arte Moderna, enjoying the gelati at his favourite café, I Caruso, or simply hiring a Lambretta and exploring off the beaten track. But something preyed on his mind and he couldn't relax and enjoy himself or barely even rest.

He had hurt someone badly. He had been thoughtless and cruel, so uncharacteristically so that it caused him great distress. He had written a letter to his friend and posted it in Dublin before boarding the ship. He had tried to explain himself, but it didn't make him feel any easier about what he'd done. The nomad in him told him he was just doing what came naturally, but his conscience told him he was running away.

He wasn't really running away, was he? After all, he had planned to take this trip in the spring of next year anyway. No, he reassured himself, he had merely brought the trip forward because he'd needed time and space.

Lots of space between himself and a love he could never return.

Chapter Eleven

Bogart hadn't been home for two days. I wasn't really concerned; tomcats do that all the time. He'd come home when he was ready. He probably had a new woman in the neighbourhood, lucky boy.

It was human company I really missed. A lover's heat, the feeling of flesh against flesh. Hot, steamy nights, when I would roll over and enjoy the sensation of the night air as it cooled my sweat-soaked skin.

I decided to run a hot bath, pour a large gin and listen to Coldplay. I was just settling in and letting the steaming water ease the strain in my cramped, aching muscles. Chris Martin's dulcet tones were washing over me and I was just about to reach for my gin when I heard the unmistakable sound of the front door opening.

'Beth,' I called out instinctively. 'Is that you?'

No answer.

'Beth? Joaquin, is that you mate?'

Only silence. The house was as still as a midnight graveyard. I stood up reluctantly, wishing that like Beth, I was in the habit of locking the door when I took a bath and was alone in the house. I sighed as I pulled on my bathrobe. I was halfway downstairs before I realised I could no longer hear the music. My iPod was docked in my bedroom next to the bathroom. That's weird, I thought, you could usually hear it in the hallway.

The front door was closed, and I checked the house from top to bottom, even the cellar beyond the basement where we stored coal and a couple of bottles of wine. There was nothing. It was empty. I ran up the cellar steps and checked the back door. It was locked.

'Bleeding hell,' I cursed.

Scouting in the 'important things draw' in the hallway table, I found the front door key and turned it in the lock until it clicked. I resented leaving my nice, warm bath and, hoping it hadn't gone cold on me, began to take the steps two at a time. Suddenly, I was overcome by a feeling of dread. I stopped dead on the stairs, my breaths coming in short, sharp blasts, misted in the ice-cold air that seemed to wrap itself around me like a living, parasitic thing, drawing all the warmth and energy from my body.

It felt as though I wasn't alone. Somebody, something was in the house with me.

I froze, unable to move, and as suddenly as it appeared, it was gone. The feeling had gone, the warmth returned to the room and I found myself able to move again. It was then that I heard it. I felt the warm breath on my neck and the hair all over my body prickled.

'Jared.'

Just once, whispered. A soft, familiar voice, a female's or a child's voice.

I ran upstairs and into the bathroom, locking the door behind me. I plunged into the warm, comforting depths of my bath, and as it closed over my head, I shut my eyes, listening only to the water pressing against my eardrums and the steady, mesmeric beat of my heart. I stayed, lost in the watery oblivion until forced up to breathe.

It took several seconds for me to realise that the music had come back on. Maybe it hadn't stopped, maybe I was going stir crazy, losing what was left of the few marbles I had. I took a large swig of gin and breathed deeply. Maybe I was drinking too much?

I relaxed back into the warmth of the bath. I could taste salt on my lips from the perspiration and feel the satisfying burn of neat gin in my throat. My favourite song was playing and I hummed along tunelessly.

The room seemed to be getting darker and I squinted incomprehensively at the bathroom window. If anything, the day had brightened slightly and the sun, although weak, was shining dead ahead. A shiver ran down my spine and I turned my head slowly and cautiously toward the bathroom door.

The top two panels were glazed with frosted glass. It was Beth's idea as the landing was too dark in winter. There against the glass panels, blocking out any light from the tiny landing window was a black silhouette. It was small, maybe that of a woman or a young boy. I instinctively stood and pulled my robe tightly around me, my heart pounding in my chest. The silhouette stayed perfectly still, not making a sound, and I felt suddenly very angry.

I jumped out of the bath and in one swift movement, unlocked and wrenched open the door, stepping out into the landing. It closed behind me with a gentle click and I moved aside toward the bedroom door.

There was nobody there! My skin prickled again, and I suddenly felt exposed and vulnerable. Two long, thin strips of light penetrated the shadowy corridor and there at the top of the stairs, glinting in the watery, autumnal sunlight, lay my wedding ring.

Chapter Twelve

Rachel

The family in Joaquin's house were a noisy bunch. He shouted, she cried and the boy, Tristan, screamed.

Early one evening, after burning my food, *again* and leaving the French doors open to clear the smoke, I heard them arguing in the back garden. From what I could make out, what with the sobbing and the screeching, was that they had lost a fortune. Same old situation. She was used to the good life and spent like there was no tomorrow. He worked all hours to accommodate this and she complained that he was never there for his family. Like I said 'same old, same old,' the difference here being her undisguised resentment and the extent of his anger.

I heard Alan in his garden, probably recycling and doing so discreetly, as though he felt uncomfortable about overhearing the fight in the neighbouring garden. I wanted to shout to him and ask if he'd seen Bogart, but I couldn't bring myself to do so in case he called me out.

Alan was very popular on Burlington Road, especially amongst the women. He was a real gentleman. Tall, distinguished and unashamedly charming, Alan was old-school, an Ian McKellen or Simon Callow type. Quietly intellectual, fiercely private, undoubtedly homosexual.

Chapter Thirteen

Alan

'You're going to die,' you tell your reflection. It's as if you're passing on the burden to someone else.

When you first learn of this you are numbed. You feel nothing. You wait for the fear that's inevitably to come. Even so, when it hits, you're not prepared for the assault.

Fear like this sneaks up on you from below. You stand still too long, like a tree, and it creeps up around you. A parasitic thing, it clings to you for sustenance and you feed it.

It invades you and once inside, it paralyses with an iron grip, like ice-cold fingers around your heart. Your lungs fight for air and your stomach knots like a ball of wool.

No-one or nothing can free a man from his fear. You're too entwined, too connected… you try to sleep, to escape…to forget.

In the morning, fear has etched its procession upon your face.

'Pity me,' you beg the man in your shaving mirror.

Chapter Fourteen

I felt really blue again, despite the Prozac. Maybe I should cut down? It didn't help it just kept me awake at nights and made my head fuzzy when I needed it to be clear. I could not handle these feelings of helplessness, of being caged. I felt suffocated, stifled. I was scaling the walls. Cabin fever had hit with a vengeance. Claustrophobic waves of panic swept through me and it was like being smothered.

I'd never felt this way before, not even in summer when the sounds of neighbours enjoying a beer in the garden and the delicious smells of barbequed meat tantalised me through the open window.

Things were starting to get strange in here too. I'd put the events of last weekend behind me; too hot a bath, combined with an empty stomach, gin and Prozac. Hell, who would take me seriously? But now things had started to move by themselves. Only this morning, I stubbed my toe on the chest of drawers in my room because it had been pulled away from the wall, and things had started to disappear, my watch, my razor…Bogart!

I was missing the cat. I never realised I was so fond of him. I kept going to the door and shouting him, but no joy. Seemed he too had decided to leave me and move on.

The nights were drawing in and I decided to make a fire. I didn't understand why the house had gone from really warm to freezing cold within a matter of days. Maybe I was coming down with something.

I texted my brother Nathan and I suddenly felt a little better. He told me Sylvia, my mother, had been trying to call and that he was glad I was still in the land of the living. I told him everything was fine and I was enjoying my own company at the moment but hoped to see him soon. The messaging session was short-lived; unlike his big brother, our Nathan has never been a man of words.

The fire, coupled with the mellow tones of Satchmo's trumpet, had its usual hypnotic effect on me. Beth had left behind her collection of nineteen-thirties blues and jazz and I enjoyed how the music made me feel.

I found myself thinking of Bogart as I drifted off, but it's Clara I dreamed of when I finally fell to sleep.

Chapter Fifteen

Clara

Clara waited nervously in the wings. This was to be her big break; at only fifteen she was to become a chorus girl at the Palais. Third row, but what the hell, everyone had to start somewhere.

Her Dad wasn't at all pleased. It was nineteen forty-four and he thought she should become a land-girl, or get a job in a 'munitions factory, like her sister Dora 'who'd gorn before her.' She suppressed a giggle. She couldn't think of anything worse and besides, everyone was saying that the war would soon be over, the allies had the Hun on the run and a job's a job as her mother would often say. Besides, they needed the money.

Her dad Bert, injured in the battle of the Somme, worked as a clerk in the offices of the local Co-operative, and her mother Fran worked all hours cleaning, sewing and laundering for whoever would pay her. But that wasn't for Clara. The stage was her calling. After all, she'd been singing and dancing for as long as she could walk and talk.

She checked herself in the dressing room mirror before heading off on stage, a few steps ahead of the other girls who pushed past her and giggled when the feathers in their head-dress brushed her face.

You would never know I was only fifteen, she thought, admiring her curvaceous body, her pert breasts and her full pout. Her shoulder-length auburn hair fell in soft curls around her face, her pretty and lightly freckled nose the only giveaway to her youth.

She caught the eye of one the technicians and blushed when he winked at her. Cheeky bugger, she thought to herself, the flush still evident on her face as she ran onstage.

Chapter Sixteen

I cursed myself for my cowardice. Bogart had been missing for over a week now and it was starting to get cold, but try as I might, I couldn't go out and look for him. Instead, I hovered about just inside the door, shouting his name and hoping to hear the familiar thud as he jumped on the fence from Victor and Margaret's garden. I left food out, but all that did was attract foxes. I had to face it, it was hopeless. All I could do was sit and wait.

It got pretty bad, the waiting. I had no idea I would miss the little man so much. It was a comfort to hear him breathing at night and he was someone to talk to. Not much of a conversationalist granted, but another living creature in the house, and now I was lost without him.

I dreamed again that night. This time it wasn't so much a frightening dream as a weird and somewhat disturbing one, like David Lynch meets Dennis Potter kind of weird.

I was young again, just a boy, and I was in my grandma's kitchen. I remember it vividly. The huge enamel range she had, from which came the delicious smell of baking bread, and my grandma herself, small, portly and dressed in a flowery overall. She had her back to me and was busying herself with making a pie. I could see the flour up her arms, and every now and then, a cloud like disturbed talcum powder flew into the air as she rolled out the pastry.

Although I was roughly that age in the late seventies, seven maybe eight, in my dream it was clearly much earlier than that. The music drifting in from the parlour was dreamy like the music they listened to during the war and my clothes were of that era too.

My grandma was singing along to the music. I can remember it clearly. *Midnight, With the Stars and You,* by Al Bowlley. I knew that because Beth had it on one of her compilations and it was used more recently as the soundtrack to the film The Shining.

Grandma had finished her pie and turned around to show it to me before she put it in the oven. But when she turned to me, she had no face. Not like it was just in shadow. She had no features at all, just skin. I screamed, but on this occasion I never woke up.

Chapter Seventeen

Graham

Graham waited in the underground car park; his car, parked in the farthest corner, was concealed by shadows. He lingered patiently, barely moving, and watched as his co-workers left one by one for the weekend and whatever lives they lived outside of the office. Was it his imagination or had they been a little bit friendlier towards him lately? Especially the new girl in reception. Now... what was her name, Laura? No... No, Lisa. That's right, Lisa.

Graham leered in the darkness. Yes, he'd noticed Lisa alright. From his desk he had a clear view of reception. He watched as she made her way across the office, photocopying or making coffee. He admired her well-kept figure. Women were generally so slovenly these days, overweight, tattooed, their hair in all manner of bizarre styles and colours. But not Lisa. She was a lady! Lisa you could take home to meet Mother.

He drooled when he thought of the tight pencil skirt that accentuated her perfect bottom, the gentle curve of her calf against the sheer fabric of her black stockings, the shadow on her thigh when her skirt rode up while sitting, hinting at the pleasures of what lay beyond.

A sudden noise distracted him from his thoughts. The car park door opened and the sound of raucous laughter filled the air, emphasised by the acoustics in the cavernous, empty space. There was Lisa, chatting with two of those harpies from Accounts and slimy Simon, the office clerk.

After what seemed an age, they finished talking about their plans for the weekend, parted and got into their cars, Lisa being the last one to pull out.

Graham clicked his seatbelt and turned on the engine, then with all the cunning of a large cat hunting its prey, he began to follow Lisa home.

Chapter Eighteen

I awoke suddenly. This was becoming a habit and not one I particularly cared for.

My heart was racing, my hands were clammy and my mouth dry. Momentarily disorientated, I searched the room, looking for any signs of familiarity to give me a clue as to my whereabouts. The room was pitch black and unnaturally cold. A pair of evil, yellow eyes glinted at me from a dark corner and I froze.

'Bogart you idiot!' I let out a sigh of relief as two pointy grey ears and a furry face appeared out of the darkness. The cat stretched, yawned and then started to wash himself before jumping on the bed. I grabbed him and held him close.

'Where have you been Sam Spade? Another case to crack?' I pretended to scold him for his absence, secretly overjoyed to see him alive and well.

'I'm going to get you done boy,' I said, stroking his ears vigorously. He purred loudly, rubbing up against my arm. 'I'm getting too old to be worrying about you, dirty stop-out.'

Suddenly he jumped, turned to face the door and then fled under the bed.

Cree-eak. SLAM!

I almost jumped out of my skin. I was guessing this was this noise that had woken me up. It seemed to come from the kitchen and at first I couldn't identify it.

Cree-eak. SLAM!

Again, this time louder. My heart in my mouth, I leaned over and reached under the bed for my cricket bat. Please let it be there. *Please*! I felt the soft pads of Bogart's paw on my hand, as if to say 'go get 'em man, I'll stay here and guard the bedroom.'

'Coward.' I smiled at him, despite my mounting fear. 'Bogart, my arse. We should have called you Scooby Poo, like I wanted to.'

I slowly got up and out of bed. Damn! It was cold. My breath misted in the frozen air.

'So much for an Indian summer,' I grumbled, as I walked downstairs in virtual darkness, only the streetlight through the landing window illuminating my way.

Creeeak. SLAM!

Damn it! I nearly ran back upstairs and got under the bed with the cat.

When I reached the bottom step, I felt with my hand along the wall. It was darker still here. The light from the street through the door panels was partially obscured by the branches of a small tree we had in the front yard, only thin slivers of light breaking through to form a gloomy orange pattern on the wall.

I walked the length of the hallway, my heart in my mouth, and stopped right outside the kitchen. I had planned an ambush. However, I ran through the kitchen wielding my cricket bat and screaming like William Wallace going into battle.

There was nobody there! I watched as the cellar door creaked open and then slammed shut again on its spring. That would explain the draught. I breathed deeply, a sigh of relief, and shot the bolt. Exactly why the cellar door would cause a horrible draught in my bedroom when the rest of the house was warm, I didn't even want to think about.

On my way back, I stopped at the landing window and looked out into the garden. There was a light shining into Joaquin's back garden from the house and I opened the window slightly. The night air was cool after the recent rain. I looked at my watch. 11.30 pm. Shit! I hadn't been asleep all that long.

The Meldrews next door were just turning in. I saw their landing light go out. Bit late for them I thought and grinned; maybe Victor had been ravishing Margaret on the sofa. Eurgh! I screwed up my face in disgust at the thought of it: her in her flowery winceyette night gown, rollers in her hair, face full of cold cream and him bare-chested and horny. Curse my over-active imagination.

Bogart had decided it was safe to leave the confines of the bed and jumped onto the windowsill to see what it was I was looking at.

'Thanks Humph.' I picked him up and he snuggled in to me. 'How I'm supposed to see anything through your oversized rump is beyond me.'

I suddenly remembered that he had no food out and carried him downstairs to the kitchen.

'Don't get used to this, fatso,' I warned him and laughed as he purred and rubbed my face with his ears, tickling my nose so that I almost dropped him. Rooting through the cupboard for his food, I saw the half empty bottle of gin and I remembered the wedding ring incident. I'd been drinking when I threw it down the waste disposal and I'd been drinking when I found it again on the landing. I yawned, pouring the dry cat food into Bogart's bowl and he tucked in hungrily.

'Later cat,' I said, turning off the kitchen light. 'Don't make too much noise when you come to bed.'

I resolved to stop taking the Prozac after today. Maybe even stop drinking?

'Ghosts indeed,' I laughed as I bounded upstairs. But I couldn't suppress a shudder as I passed the bathroom door.

Chapter Nineteen

Alan

You have an inoperable, non-malignant tumour. Diagnosis, terminal. The tumour is growing at an alarming rate and in doing so is pressing against certain nerves and receptors in your brain, gradually cutting off the blood supply.

It could go either way. A couple of inches to left could see you suffering a severe depression of mind and senses. As it is, you feel euphoric! You are seeing the world through new eyes. Colours are vivid and bright, everything is sharp and well defined, at the same time ghosted and fuzzy-edged almost like an after-thought.

Your senses are heightened. Smell, taste… At the slightest touch, your skin feels exquisite pleasure. Even the blandest of foods leave your taste buds dancing. *You can see the vein of the leaf, pulsating with life!*

But the strangest side effect of all is your new-found ability to smell emotions. You can smell your own fear, a damp, earthy, cloying smell that it hits you like waves of nausea. Your chemically induced happiness smells of lemon-scented cucumber and summer days.

You hear long before you see the tiny padding of the robin's foot on top of your fence as he delights in tormenting your neighbour's cat.

You wish you didn't have to die.

Chapter Twenty

'Of all the gin joints, in all the towns, in all the world, she had to walk into mine.'

It was three a.m. The ungodly hour when everyone seemed to be sleeping, except me. I was curled up on the sofa with Bogart, watching his namesake on Turner classic movies.

Watching *with* Bogart meant *I* was watching Casablanca and he was asleep, whiskers twitching with a big, fat Cheshire cat grin on his face. Probably dreaming of the feline version of Ingrid Bergman or Lauren Bacall. The reason I was 'curled up' is that he was stretched out his full length, occupying two thirds of the sofa.

I couldn't help but think how cool Bogart was. The real Bogart that is, not the snoring, be-whiskered fleabag by my side. What would he do in my situation, the smouldering, brooding hero? Beat up the bad guys and win back the broad and all with an air of menace and sophistication.

You had to hand it to him. Like many Hollywood idols of his era, the guy oozed class. Most of them did back then, only Bogart more so somehow. Women who weren't even born when he died fell in love with him after watching his films, and Beth was one of them.

Beth and I first met at university. Some students were throwing a freshers party themed 'Stars of the silver screen' and myself and some equally dull friends had decided to play it safe and go as The Lone Ranger, Tonto and Silver, completely missing the point of being the star and not their famous characters.

Guess who drew the short straw and had to spend the night stifling hot and embarrassed in a papier mache horse head?

Beth was resplendent as Greta Garbo. Her short dark curls had been waxed into a thirties style crop, and she wore an authentic man's suit of the era, which fitted her as though she'd had it tailored. Her large, beautiful green eyes were framed with long sweeping lashes beneath perfectly arched, pencil-thin eyebrows, and her lips were full and painted flaming red.

I spent the evening gazing at her from the corner. Watching as every man at the party tried to win her over. In the end, *she* came over to me.

'Hey Silver,' she said, laughing and tapping on the headpiece with a dangerously long and pointed red nail. 'So, who's the mystery man beneath the mask?'

'Hey Dietrich,' I said removing the mask, my face flushed and burning. 'I'm Jared, Jared Colne.' She laughed again.

'I'm Garbo,' she purred. 'But as it's hardly an insult, I'll forgive you.'

The rest, as they say, is history. We were soon a regular couple. I could hardly believe my luck and neither could anyone else. She was so beautiful and so clever.

By the time we left university, we were already engaged.

Chapter Twenty One

Clara

Clara stood beneath the stage-door in the alleyway, under a canopy that had been built during the war for the black-out. It might have kept the Germans at bay, but it barely kept out the chill, she thought, stamping her feet to keep warm. Her breath misted in the still night air as she sighed. Her auburn hair burnished red in the melancholic glow of the stage-door light. It was a damp, misty night and she hugged her faux mink stole close against the cold.

It was well after midnight and she'd long since finished her show at the Palais. Front row no less, in under a year. She smiled to herself, but its radiance was lost as she stepped back into the shadows. I'll soon be lead, she thought. Star of the show. Mr. Willis the production manager had hinted as much. He was really pleased with her singing and she was certain her new admirer had put in a good word. After all, he was an influential man, wasn't he?

Where is that man? she wondered. A tremor of excitement ran through her body at the thought of meeting him. All evening he had plied her with champagne via the bartender, never once approaching her. It was real champagne too, not the cheap stuff. He sat in shadow at end of the bar, silhouetted by the spotlights, his eyes shaded by the brim of his fedora. Just like Jimmy Cagney, she thought and smiled.

She lit a cigarette, using a cheap Bakelite holder to keep it from marking her elbow-length satin gloves with ash. Her crimson lips were aflame in the illumination of the match. She looked again at the message scrawled on the back of the match book.

'Meet me by the stage door after hours.' So where was he?

A sleek, black limousine pulled up beside the kerb at the top of the alleyway, and the back window lowered an inch or so.

'Miss Taylor?' a disembodied voice said from somewhere within, a deep velvet voice that sent shivers up and down her spine. She let the un-smoked cigarette fall from its holder, crushing it into the sodden ground with her foot as she walked unhurriedly towards the open car door.

Chapter Twenty Two

I woke up around four, cold and cramped. Bogart had gone, presumably to bed, and the fire had long since died down. As I stood, my bones creaked in protest and my muscles ached in places I didn't know I had places.

Something drew my attention to the window. It wasn't a noise, but an inexplicable feeling that someone was out there, watching. Fed up of feeling spooked, I made bold to the window and peered out. There, beneath the streetlight opposite stood a boy of around fourteen. A strange, pale, no *grey*-faced boy, for whom the melancholy orange glow of the lamp did no favours, giving his skin a waxy un-natural appearance.

Again I felt the hair rising all over my body, as if someone were blowing cold air down my neck, and fear held me tight in its grip, as though my legs were clamped in irons. A fear without real foundation, for although the boy stared unblinkingly at me, an attitude characteristic now of a lad his age being watched by someone through the window, he was after all just a boy.

You may have figured out by now that I was not the bravest of souls, but not even I would stand rooted to the spot with fear because of a young lad, however leery. But this lad was different; there was something unearthly about him. I stared into his pale eyes transfixed and as I watched, he silently mouthed a word at me.

A word I heard inside my head, a word I heard inside the room, as clearly as if he'd been standing next to me.

Just one word… *Jared.*

The next day I was filled with a resolve to make changes. I would cut out the drinking, cut down, gradually filtering out the pills and I would make a call, just one phone call a day, just to make contact with the outside world again. I plugged the phone in cautiously. I remembered how Joaquin had a really old phone and he'd taken the bell out of it so no-one could disturb him, picking it up occasionally to check if anyone was there. So if you needed him you might just get lucky and connect at the same time.

I turned the handset to silent mode, so I wouldn't get startled and I could control who I spoke to and when. I wondered who I should call first. Not my mother. I needed to work up to that one. She never did like Beth and she would waste no time in telling me so, and that was the last thing I needed.

I found myself calling Joaquin's number. A woman's voice answered and I dropped the phone in shock. I hadn't expected anyone to reply. Then I realised it must be the people who'd moved in to number thirty-seven, the Sloanes. They must have kept the same number.

I was furious with myself. I should have a least apologised, said I had the wrong number; at least it was a connection. What an idiot! What the hell was wrong with me? I'd never been scared of the phone before.

'Right!' I told Bogart, who was sat on the arm of the sofa, regarding me with undisguised contempt, as is a cat's wont. 'I'm calling for a take-away.'

Bogart yawned, stretched and turned his back to me as I dialled. I had a long wait for the pizza parlour to pick up, which was no bad thing I initially thought, as it gave me time to collect my wits. But as time passed I started to get nervous. I was about to hang up when I heard a voice at the other end.

'Hello, Pizza Parade. Gemma speaking. How may I help you?'

'H-h-hello,' I stammered. 'Could I order a p-pizza, please?' I heard Gemma sigh impatiently on the other end.

'What kind of pizza would that be, sir?'

'Any, erm meat, any meat, no fish...' Gemma said something to a colleague and I heard her giggle. I nearly dropped the phone but a sharp look from Bogart, who had heard the word 'pizza,' and my resolve came back.

'Meat feast special, sir?' said Gemma automatically. 'What size?'

'Your biggest,' I said, finally finding my tongue. 'And chicken wings and a bottle of coke.' I managed to give out my address, I even managed a somewhat sarcastic 'Thank you, Gemma' before hanging up.

'Yes!' I punched the air and Bogart raised an eyebrow at me sardonically.

The relief I felt was instantaneous. It was like I'd been walking around all summer in the baking heat and I'd finally been able to remove my winter overcoat. I was about to try going into the garden, but something stopped me.

'One step at a time Jared,' I reproached myself. 'One step at a time.'

Still I was mighty proud of myself at that.

Chapter Twenty Three

Graham

The moon broke through the cloud cover, partially obscured by wispy tendrils that she wore like a chiffon scarf against a bone-white evening gown. Everything was bathed in her silvery glow, and the remnants of an earlier shower clung to the windscreen like a thousand sparkling diamonds.

Graham had sat patiently across the street from Lisa's flat for a good couple of hours now, watching and waiting, for what? Not even he knew. He just loved the proximity, the closeness to the woman he had fallen in love with, and he just knew that for once his feelings were reciprocated. Hadn't she given him a lovely smile only yesterday as she stood waiting for the photocopier while he bought coffee from the nearby machine?

Graham had felt lost and desperately lonely for most of his life. True enough he had his mother, but it wasn't the same as having a real woman. Not someone he could hold and love, someone to fill the gap in his otherwise empty life. Lisa's existence had filled that gap for him. True she was just a colleague, someone he saw in the office, but seeing her there somehow made his life bearable. Even his working life.

He had narrowly escaped redundancy this time. He heard David, the office clown, telling the other clerks that although Slimy Simon was far more competent, he was the one who would have to go, as it would cost them tens of thousands in severance to let Graham go. They had all sniggered as he walked past, but he no longer cared.

He sat at his desk and his gaze wandered across to Lisa. Two of his colleagues noticed. They nudged one another and giggled, but it was water off a duck's back to Graham. It barely even registered.

Back in the car, he held his breath as a couple walked by suspiciously close to the vehicle and tried to look in, only the steam on the windows preventing them from doing so. He could barely see out himself anymore and was just about to lower the window to de-mist when they'd walked passed.

He yawned to himself and looked at the clock on the dash. Almost nine-thirty. He'd been daydreaming beneath Lisa's window for most of the evening. His mother would be furious.

'Goodnight, my love,' he mouthed up to her window as the car pulled away.

Chapter Twenty Four

Looking back, all of the signs were there with Beth.

'Our relationship is going nowhere,' she announced one day over breakfast. I looked up from my newspaper.

'Where did that come from?' I replied, bemused by the suddenness of her statement.

'I just feel we're in a rut,' she said, looking down at her cereal bowl.

'Beth we're married! Where else can we go? The next logical step is children; you don't want a baby do you? Beth, are you pregnant?'

'No!' She snapped. 'And thank God for small mercies, it would be like a sticking plaster holding together a severed limb.' I was dumbstruck at the violent reaction.

'Beth, I didn't realise you were so unhappy. When did this happen? Baby, talk to me.' Beth sighed and reached for her jacket.

'And that, Jared, is precisely what I mean.'

Chapter Twenty Five

Beth

Beth sat outside the bar with her coffee and lit a cigarette. The midday sun was warm for the time of year, but a cool north wind made the day seem chillier than it actually was.

At thirty-six she was every bit as attractive as she was when she had first married. Her chestnut hair fell to her shoulders in loose curls and her figure was trim and well kept, the dark circles beneath her eyes, the only tell-tale sign that all was not well.

She dragged on the cigarette and sighed, wondering what Jared would say if he saw her smoking again. At the thought of Jared she felt irrepressibly sad. Not the intense pain that used to plague her during the many sleepless nights when she had first left him. It was more like an ache now that wearies the soul, or the sadness one might feel while listening to a particular piece of music that stirs memories, brings back recollections, a remembered pain.

She sipped her coffee, the burning sting on her lips allowing her a momentary release from her thoughts.

'Jared, Jared, Jared,' she said out loud, automatically rubbing her stomach, as she did whenever she thought of her soon to be ex-husband and the child she had aborted. Their child. What would he say if he knew she had murdered their first and only child? How could he possibly hate her anymore than she hated herself?

Her solicitor had told her that Jared hadn't been answering his letters, which would mean she would have to pay him a visit. Still, she owed him that at least. An explanation, some kind of closure.

A woman came out of the café bar with a toddler in a pushchair. He was rosy-cheeked with a head of blond curls and he made her think of photographs she'd seen of how Jared had looked at that age. The boy smiled at Beth, and with a heavy heart she returned his smile, fighting back tears that were of late never too far from the surface.

Chapter Twenty Six

I spent long hours during that autumn just staring out of the window. When I wasn't looking out at the street at the comings and goings, I was at the back watching nature work its magic on the garden.

The lawn was overgrown after months of neglect, but not without its charms. It looked to me like a magic cottage garden, wild and unkempt, scattered with fallen leaves, the occasional wild flower adding to the vibrancy.

Bogart loved it. He was a big cat, hunting his prey in his own personal jungle, and woe betide any falling leaf or seed-head that fell into his path. I was particularly amused by one cheeky cock-robin who would sit on top of the fence and torment him, knowing full well that the cat was far too fat and lazy to chase him. Bogart would just sit on the path and tick him off, while his feathered foe mocked him from a safe distance.

The log store had toppled and some logs had rolled onto the grass, and I noticed, not without satisfaction, that Beth's expensive potted plants and herb garden had succumbed to neglect and perished. Looking out at my shed, I remembered last autumn. Beth had done whatever it is gardeners do to make good for the coming winter. She'd pruned, removed dead plants and planted some winter flowers and shrubs in pots. I'd mown the lawn, grudgingly, and then cheered up when she told me it would be the last time for that year.

I'd also sprayed the fence and the shed in preparation for the bad weather, and later we'd pulled out the barbeque for what must have been the last time. Beth opened a bottle of wine we'd bought in France, and we cuddled up on the swing and planned our future as we watched the lazy autumn sun sink into the darkening landscape.

Five months later, Beth had gone.

I suddenly felt very alone and blue. I closed the curtains on the coming night and, reaching for the Prozac, swallowed three in succession and washed them down with a tumbler of neat gin.

Chapter Twenty Seven

Alan

You called the undertaker this morning to make the final arrangements. He cannot hide his surprise at the fact that you are arranging your own funeral.

'I am alone.' You tell him without emotion.

You walk through the park and tick off a couple of young lads who are scaring the ducks with their remote controlled boat. You suppress a smile as they extend you the middle finger when they believe your back is turned.

You are happy to have seen another autumn, your favourite of all the seasons. The colours of the leaves you wade through are kaleidoscopic and effervescent in rich, warm shades of gold, red and amber. The grass looks no less verdant to you for having lost its summer vibrancy. You can smell wood smoke from the nearby railway cottages. You can hear squirrels foraging in the trees

Nature is dying off in readiness for her re-birth in spring and you feel a connectedness with her. Her beauty stirs you like no woman ever could. You are aware of your heightened sensuality and the re-awakening of your libido.

You have never felt so alive!

Chapter Twenty Eight

Rachel

Rachel sighed as she picked up her husband's trousers from where he had left them on the bathroom floor. She straightened up and looked at her reflection in the mirror. Although the bruises had faded beneath her eye and across her cheek, the memory of them lingered and the tenderness when she touched her skin remained.

Why had he behaved like that towards her? Theirs had always been an obsessive marriage. Their fights were zealous and often, the making up heated and passionate. But he had never resorted to violence before.

Why was he so angry with her? She wasn't the one who had jeopardised their livelihood. No, he had done that! Simeon Fordham and his arrogance. Now it was his pride that was costing them their marriage. There was no question of it; she would have left by now if it wasn't for their son. Rachel was not the kind of wife to tolerate being browbeaten or downtrodden. She had made it clear from the start, long before their marriage, that any abuse on his part would result in his balls being hung from their bedroom wall like a hunting trophy.

He had always loved Rachel's fire. Her passion and fighting spirit, much tamed now since the birth of Tristan. She had mellowed, softened since becoming a mother, not so much though that she would allow herself to be beaten by her spouse ever again.

They had met in a wine bar nine years ago. Rachel was meeting a client there. She was in real estate at the time. An ardent business woman she had built up her own agency by the time she was twenty-three. Simeon was in the bar with a stag party, and from the moment she had set eyes on him, she was determined to make him hers.

Staying on at the bar after her client had left, she had decided to play the long game. She had marched up to Simeon's friend at the bar, taken a double shot from his hand, necked it and then walked calmly into the toilet. After a while she walked back to her seat and played the same trick on another of his friends, completely ignoring Simeon, who could only stare after her open mouthed. It did the trick and Simeon followed her over, determined this feisty woman was the one for him.

Rachel's eyes misted over just for a second as the ringing of Simeon's mobile brought her back to her senses. She reached into the pocket of his trousers for the phone. Her husband used the same number for business as he did for his personal mobile and she thought the call might be important. The name Jono lit up on the handset, puzzling Rachel.

'Who the hell is Jono?' she thought aloud. 'I don't know any Jono.'

Swiping the screen to unlock the handset, she said, 'Simeon Fordham's—' There was a sharp intake of breath from the other end and then silence.

'Hello!' The call was cut off from the other end. Rachel held the phone to her ear for a moment, catching a glimpse of her reflection in the mirror, before placing the handset back in her husband's trouser pocket.

Her beautiful features hardened into a grimace, and the narrow eyes that stared back at her glinted dangerously in the glow.

Chapter Twenty Nine

'Hello Sylvia. It's me, Jared.'

Experience had taught me to hold the phone well away from my ear when phoning my mother, but the unexpected silence on the other end of the line unnerved me even more. Let me explain. My mother hated my wife and not just with the usual 'you're not good enough for my boy' resentment. She *really* hated her and I never understood why. I had always supposed it was because Beth was the only person I know of to ever stand up to her, apparently when Sylvia had warned Beth at our engagement party that she would marry her son 'over her dead body.'

'So be it,' Beth had retorted.

Thus began the clash of the titans!

'How are you, Jared?' my mother said, her voice dull and un-emotive. 'It's been a while.'

'Yes. Yes it has. I'm sorry I haven't been calling, but I needed space to clear my head.'

'Leaving us in the dark and worried about you no less,' she continued. 'Anyhow you're fine now, so how about lunch on Sunday?'

'Fine now!' Her words made me smile. I was fine now. She made it sound as if I had had a wart removed. There were times when I wondered if I would ever be 'fine' again.
The silence hung between us. A pregnant pause. Sylvia awaited her answer on the other end of the line.

My heart pounded. Lunch on Sunday. How I would get around this one?

'Why don't you come to me?' I said, instantly regretting it. I knew my mother would have plenty to say about my circumstances, not least about the house and the way I'd been living.

I asked after Dad, and then I hung up and breathed a sigh of relief. The ice had been broken but I was already dreading Sunday.

Chapter Thirty

Clara

Clara leaned over the bridge and stared into the deep, turbulent waters. It would be so easy she thought, so quick and easy. She imagined falling into the river the initial shock of the ice cold water on her skin, the thunderous rush of the flow in her ears.

She imagined surrendering herself to the pull, being swallowed, sinking into the abyss like falling into a deep sleep. It would be calm down there, she reflected. Calm and peaceful and green, like a meadow in summertime.

She pictured the last breath of air escaping from her laboured lungs, a bubble of kaleidoscope colours, pausing a while on her lips before being carried away by the current… And then she pictured the light. The beautiful and brilliant golden-white light that is the beginning and the end of all things. A flutter in her stomach brought her back to earth with a bang.

At only seventeen years of age, her life was over! Her career on stage finished. At only seventeen she was carrying the child of a married man. She'd known he was married all along, of course she had. The indentation on his finger where his wedding ring had been, the covert manner in which he lived his double life, his real life with his wife and daughter and his life with her. She knew he had a wife and daughter, she'd seen them together in a magazine. He was someone, this man! Only last night she'd seen him in a film, playing the villain to Kenneth More's hero.

He was meant to be someone who could launch her career in stage and screen, but as it was, he was the one who had brought it to a premature end. Even without the child, she knew that doors were closing to her.

His agent, who had all along been acting as go-between for the couple, had warned her as much. No-one would believe a starlet's word over his. She would be branded a liar at best, a whore and home-wrecker by his fans the world over. She knew how the world looked upon such women.

Two years on stage had made her wise beyond her years, but clearly she still had so much to learn.

Again she felt the fluttering in her stomach as light and gentle as a butterfly's wings. She looked for one last time over the bridge, her tears falling and mingling with the swell.

'Time to face the consequences, girl,' she sniffed, rubbing her swollen belly.

Chapter Thirty One

The world of weird had increased somewhat over the last week or so. I was sat having a coffee yesterday, doing my online shopping in preparation for Sunday, when the light in the kitchen dimmed and then brightened, dimmed, brightened once more and then exploded. I don't mean it popped. I mean it literally exploded with a hiss and a loud bang, showering me with tiny fragments of glass.

My missing watch turned up in Bogart's scratching post tunnel and unless he's part magpie, I don't understand how it could have got there. He hadn't used that tunnel since kitten-hood; he was too fat to even fit in there.

The cellar door kept unlocking itself and banging in the night. Bogart ignored it but I had to go down and shut it. I resolved to look in my man draw in the old larder for a padlock, but I hadn't done it, the main reason being that if the door unbolted itself in the middle of the night, I would surely be calling for the priest. That is if I didn't have a fear-induced heart attack first. At least until I changed it, I could reason that the ancient lock was to blame for the door swinging open.

I had never really believed in ghosts, but I found myself seeing shadows everywhere. Things that moved and you just happened to catch them from the corner of your eye.

I even looked online at the page of a mystic agony aunt. She advised people to 'communicate' with their spirits to find out what they wanted. Not for me methinks!

Thankfully I hadn't had another bathroom episode, and nor had I seen the boy since, so I'd just put the feelings of being watched down to stress and depression. Stress due to my mother's impending visit and depression at being confined to the house.

Later, exhausted as I was after giving the house a good going over in preparation for Sunday, I was enjoying a peaceful, dreamless afternoon nap when I was rudely awakened by the sound of a siren in the street. For some reason I thought of Clara, but when I rushed to the window, I saw the ambulance outside of number forty-two. Graham was hovering in the doorway, his face expressionless as he watched his mother being wheeled into the ambulance.

My imagination was in overdrive. I knew Graham was a little odd but surely he wouldn't hurt his own mother? I thought of Sylvia and how suffocating she was. I couldn't begin to imagine living with her all my life. I thought I'd probably drown myself in the tub.

Graham stood and watched as the ambulance drove away and then, closing the front door firmly behind him, he got into his car and made off in the opposite direction.

Chapter Thirty Two

Alan

You dreamed of your love last night. His twinkling, Irish eyes and his thick mane of dark curls. In your dreams you shared a private joke, laughing together and shutting out the rest of the world. When you woke you could smell the warm, buttery, caramel smell of love on your pillow!

You awaken regularly in the wee, small hours. Forgetful for a moment or two about the time-bomb ticking away in your head. It's a desolate and lonely feeling when the realisation hits, usually with the dawning of a new day, but with each new day the feelings of fear and desolation diminish a little more, until acceptance finally finds you and cocoons you in a blanket of peace.

All of a sudden it's ok to die; actually, it's imperative!

You have no family. Both your parents are dead so your mourners will be few, your friends beating a hasty retreat after your diagnosis, as though death just by its mentioning is contagious.

Three nights ago you had a conversation with your long-deceased grandmother as she sat at the foot of your bed.

'We love you Alan,' she told you with vacant eyes. 'And we are waiting for you.'

Never have the stars shone so brightly. The night sky is resplendent in hues of purple and blue.

You see the boy again, stood beneath the streetlamp. Jared's boy. He sees you and smiles, and although his lips never move, you can hear his thoughts.

You know Jared is alone now. You hear his midnight sighs through the wall; you can smell his sadness like wet wool or old baby clothes that still carry a trace of the scent of a newborn. You know he is alone, and in your darker moments you think of him and share his pain.

Chapter Thirty Three

Joaquin

Joaquin walked down to the quay at Porto Civitavecchia. He squinted against the bright sun, but despite the moderate climate of the Italian autumn, he felt a chill come over him, as though he'd just stepped out of the baking sun and into the shade.

At passport control he gave up his passport and ship's documentation for inspection. There were three pretty Italian girls working in a nearby office who eyed him appreciatively, calling out to him and giggling as he passed. The deep frown that marred his handsome face implied that he hadn't appreciated the gesture. In reality, he hadn't even noticed.

Overhead the sky was a perfect cornflower blue; the few white clouds there tumbled over each other, a continuous, playful movement blown along by the gentle coastal breeze. He looked back out to sea at the storm clouds that were gathering on the horizon and they looked ominous. He shuddered; he could not shake the anxious feeling that had weighed him down over the last couple of days. He felt drained, like he was coming down with something. It was hard work aboard a cargo ship, but he was fit and strong and it was nothing unusual to him. No, his was an inner weariness. A nervy, ailing fatigue of the mind and he couldn't shake it.

He was unusually tetchy too. Some of the men had been teasing him about losing at cards, and this had led to more teasing, this time about his hair. One had asked when he was having the operation and another had said that he was perhaps in the closet. This led to a homophobic onslaught, and fuelled by alcohol, it had nearly come to blows.

Joaquin was a pacifist. He hated violence. He was also a master of martial arts, having no less than three black belts and six dans over three different disciplines. Last night he was heading towards losing control and he dreaded to think of the outcome had one of the lads challenged him. He hadn't been drunk, far from it, but he felt agitated and tense. What the hell was wrong with him?

He was thinking about his friend Alan and the dream he'd had last night. In the dream, Alan and he had been hiking across rough terrain and were walking back beside a river, sharing a joke and looking forward to a well-earned pint. Then the dream had turned dark and suddenly he was stood over the dead body of his friend. Alan's face had been twisted, contorted with fear, and Joaquin woke up in a cold sweat, horrified and troubled by the dream. His anxiety had gradually increased since.

Truth be known, he'd thought of little else since Alan's admission of love had caused him to flee Burlington Road. It wasn't that he was homophobic or that he'd never been the subject of male admiration before. He had many gay friends and was confident enough in his sexuality to be flattered by the attention.

Alan was a dear friend from way back, and his love had to be deep and genuinely felt or he would never have felt the need to confess to Joaquin. They had never discussed his homosexuality before. It was a given and it didn't matter a fig to Joaquin, who would have happily befriended an alien given the opportunity.

He knew that all Alan needed was the reassurance that it would not affect their friendship. He knew that Alan didn't expect him to return his declaration of love or discuss such an eventuality. What Alan hadn't expected was for Joaquin to make his excuses and flee the country. In doing so, Joaquin had not only offended his friend but hurt him deeply in the process.

What Alan didn't know, however, was that Joaquin was not disgusted by the declaration. Anyone would be flattered by Alan's attention. It was the thought of being loved that had terrified Joaquin, not the thought of being loved by *Alan.*

Had he really distanced himself so far from humanity that the thought of love and commitment horrified him?

Joaquin stopped and removed his rucksack. Having so few personal possessions, he always carried them with him. He removed a bottle of water and drank from it, studying the bustle outside of the port's main terminal. He wiped his brow as though trying to remove the lasting image of his friend's death mask from his mind. Seconds later he was in the back of a taxi.

'Aeroporto di Fiumicino per favore.' He told the driver.

Chapter Thirty Four

'Ok, Sylvia, that's fine, no problem. I'll catch up with you next week. Give my love to Dad and I hope he feels better soon.'

I felt an inexplicable sense of relief when I put the phone down, closely followed by a feeling of isolation, more intense than I had ever felt before. The house around me was silent, a cloying heavy silence, like when you're underwater and can hear your own heartbeat.

Relieved as I was that Sylvia was pulling out of our family dinner thanks to Dad's man flu, I suddenly felt as if I was the only person left on the planet. My mind was in a strange place and became flooded with conflicting emotions - grief, paranoia, fear and the intolerable feeling of loneliness. On top of this though, I felt relief and also strangely peaceful.

Yes, I felt alone and nervy bordering on fearful, but these emotions were familiar bed fellows, and I found it almost comforting that my peace was not to be shattered or my sanctum invaded. I realised that loneliness and fear were my allies and that I needed my pain. That somehow through these emotions, however unhealthy, I had found a kind of equilibrium.

I scratched my stubbly chin and thought about having a shave. From the kitchen came the regular sounds of Bogart, padding around on the tiled floor looking for scraps. Through the open window I could hear Victor Meldrew next door, trimming his hedges. Everything was familiar. Everything seemed safe. It was a beautiful autumnal day, and I found myself whistling as I ran upstairs and into the bathroom.

I filled the sink with hot water and studied myself in the mirror amid the swirling steam. Recently, I'd started looking older and more tired. My dirty blond hair was beginning to curl in the neck and around my ears. Strange it had grown so fast! When Beth first left I had shaved my head smooth. Somehow, seeing a stranger in the mirror meant I didn't have to identify with his situation. Now it looked messy and unkempt, and I made a mental note to try and find one of those mobile stylists that would come to the house.

I studied the new lines on my face and the shadows beneath my eyes, soon losing myself to the steam and as the mirror misted, I found myself staring at the swirling shapes that formed in the haze.

Suddenly I felt the familiar paralysis of fear! I stood transfixed as letters began to form on the glass.

Z-A-C-H-A-R-Y.

Zachary! My mouth felt dry, the hair began to prickle on the back of my neck, and icy shivers ran down my spine. I felt instinctively that someone was standing behind me and I knew it was the boy. Suddenly the word began to fade as the mist in the mirror began to clear and I could see shapes forming in the steam behind me, a leg here, an arm there, and then a head began to form. I wanted to turn and run, to be away from this aberration that was taking place, but I couldn't move, nor even blink.

My fear rose when a face began to form in the swirling haze, vague at first but soon becoming clearer, more fleshed out. It was then I wondered how anyone could endure such horror and still be alive.

The terror reached new heights when a face formed on the ghostly boy that I knew like my own.

Chapter Thirty Five

The Meldrews

Margaret didn't want to go to Jeremy's cousin's wedding in Harrogate! Nor did she want to stop off on the coast on the way back, in their little mobile home from home.

She didn't want to walk the dogs every morning; truth be known she hated the bloody things!

She didn't want to watch Countdown with her husband or have afternoon tea, play bridge on Sunday evenings or make jam for the Women's Institute's annual fete. She didn't want Sunday roast, freshly pruned roses, a life insurance plan and matching Parker pens, Strictly Come Dancing, hypertension pills and fondue, recipes for Beef Wellington, Cosyfeet shoes or Teflon coated steam irons!

Margaret wanted to run naked on an exotic beach, ride a Harley Davidson stinking drunk down Route 66, smoke pot and listen to Nirvana. She wanted to shoplift in Harrods's, have sex with a stranger in a cinema, burn down Jeremy's shed, poison the dogs and swear at the vicar's wife…

Margaret wanted to scream!

Instead she spread the butter and home-made jam on her husband's scone, *not too thickly dear,* and tried hard to resist the urge to spit on it.

'I thought we might stop off at the coast on the way back from the wedding, dear,' said her husband, finishing off the Times crossword with exactly five minutes to spare before Gardener's Question Time.

'Make a nice change dear.' She smiled sweetly, placing Jeremy's scone and pot of Darjeeling on a tray on his lap, trying hard not to fall over the scrawny, rat-like creatures, who were begging for crumbs at his feet.

Chapter Thirty Six

I was in a world of my own, sitting at the kitchen table when a sharp tap on the window brought me back with a start. I stared dumbly at the figure standing there, my heart pounding, wondering if it wasn't another ghost, because I was certain by now that my house, myself, or both were haunted.

It took a while for me to realise who the desperate looking female tapping on my window was. It was Mrs. Dolce and Gabbana from number thirty-seven, and I ran to the kitchen door to see what she wanted.

'Please,' she said, pushing past me into the kitchen, the fear evident in her voice. 'I have to get out of there. I think he wants to kill me!'

She sat at the kitchen table. Bogart jumped up and sat purring on her knee. I would have normally pushed him off, but she seemed to get great comfort from him, so I let him stay.

'I'm sorry to intrude, but I had nowhere else to go.'

'Tea?' I said.

I studied her as she sipped and crooned over the cat. She seemed around my age or a little younger and was extremely attractive. I suddenly felt unkempt and scruffy, lounging around in my combats and an old Rolling Stones t-shirt.

I didn't ask, nor did I prompt her to tell me why she was in such a state, or why she thought someone wanted to kill her. I let her sit, drinking her tea and stroking Bogart, who was more than happy with the attention, until she calmed down. Eventually she sighed and a large tear rolled down her face.

'I'm Jared, by the way. Jared Colne,' I said a little embarrassed. I was never any good with crying women, or any women for that matter.

She sniffed. 'Sorry, I'm Rachel.' She extended a perfectly manicured hand and I shook it. 'I live at number thirty-seven.'

'I was just having a snack, Rachel, nothing special, cheese on toast, but you're welcome to join me.'

She smiled. 'Thanks, but I'm fine. I'm sorry to disturb you; I'll be out of your way soon.'

Several minutes passed and still she sat huddled over the dregs in her cup. Bogart, bored with her attention had gone off to bed. I'm not sure she even noticed.

'So, how are you finding life on Burlington Road?' I asked, desperate to start some kind of conversation.

Suddenly she burst into tears, sobbing as though her heart would break. In between sobs and one man-sized pack of tissues later, she blurted out her story.

She and her husband Simeon were on the brink of separation. It was a familiar story. He was something big in the city apparently, and he was involved in a takeover bid for an international conglomerate a couple of years back, buying up every available share for his client. He even invested himself. The shares crashed overnight losing his client millions.

He lost everything; he nearly lost the shirt on his back. They had to sell their lavish Kensington apartment and downgrade to a more modest semi, here on Burlington. There were worse places to be, but Simeon had almost died of shame. Their friends beat a hasty retreat after the move, and he blamed Rachel and her fondness for the platinum card for their situation.

Things had gotten worse recently, when young 'Tris' had to be pulled out of his private school in Westminster due to lack of funds and was looking to be placed in a state school.

To be honest, it wasn't anything I hadn't picked up from overhearing conversations in their garden. What I didn't realise though was that Simeon had admitted to having an affair.

'Are you married, Jared?'

'Erm no, that is… well to be honest, she left me around six months ago. I think she wants a divorce.' Rachel studied me hard and I noticed what beautiful, deep-set blue eyes she had.

'I'm sorry to hear that. I really am.'

'Listen,' I said, trying to tear myself away from those hypnotic eyes. 'How about something stronger? I know I could do with one.'

Rachel stood and followed me into the lounge. I hastily threw aside some dirty laundry I'd left lying around and she sat on the sofa, the faint trace of a smile never leaving her face. I wondered whether she was bemused, perhaps amused at how the other half lived. I didn't really care; much as I loved Bogart, I'd forgotten how good human company felt.

'So, what can I get you? I'm having gin, but there's wine if you'd prefer or…'

'I'll have a large g&t please,' she said, uncrossing her legs and smoothing down her immaculately sleek, chestnut bob. 'Easy on the t.'

'G&T coming up' I said, trying hard not to stare at those long, bronzed legs, which were now stretched out full length. I thought of putting some music on. My I-pod was docked and switched to random. I pressed play.

'Mmm, Cohen,' she purred. 'Sorry do you mind if I take off my shoes? They're really pinching.'

She had suddenly acquired all of the predatory traits of a woman who has her man in her sights. She kicked off her Jimmy Choo Cuban heels and began to massage her perfectly toned calf. I noticed the bruising up her arm as she did so, and she hastily pulled down her sleeve to cover it.

She soon drained her glass and I noticed her hands were still a little shaky. I asked her if she was ok and she looked close to tears again. Two thirds of a bottle of Tanquerey later, (she'd dispensed with the tonic after the first glass) found her curled up on the sofa, those perfect legs tucked beneath her, listening to me pouring my heart out about Beth, Joaquin, my mother and being confined to the house. I didn't mention the spook-in-residence for fear she'd either think me insane or that I would frighten her off.

Rachel listened intently, not interrupting until I'd finished, her solemn eyes unblinking, yet somehow gentle and sincere in their intensity. When I stopped speaking she laughed, and I looked at her, bemused.

'I'm sorry,' she said, trying to suppress her amusement. 'I'm not laughing at you honestly. I've just realised what a pathetic pair we are. Maybe we should join forces?' she added mischievously, with a twinkle in those beautiful eyes. 'Really though Mr. Colne, Leonard Cohen and Tanquerey are hardly the right medicine for the blues.'

I suddenly saw the funny side of it. I laughed and she laughed, both of us hugging our sides until tears streamed down our faces, and I realised that I hadn't laughed that way for a long, long time.

'Let's dance,' she said, suddenly jumping up. I looked at her as if she were mad. 'C'mon, Jared.' She smiled, reaching for my hand. 'Dance me to the end of love.'

She fell into me, already well cut, and I held her there to prevent her from falling.

'Why thank-you kind sir' she said, looking into my eyes. As she reached up to peck my cheek, my mouth brushed hers and I could taste the gin on her lips. We both pulled back as if startled.

'Wow!' she said, still laughing. 'Now, there's a bonus.' She pressed against me and I felt myself growing hard. I drew away slightly, feeling a little embarrassed, but she snuggled into me, resting her head on my shoulder, and I could smell her scent, her hair, her womanliness. I began stroking her head, caressing her back and the nape of her neck and she murmured slightly, Cohen's velvet doing what Cohen's velvet does.

Suddenly, she looked up at me and for a split second I saw fear in her eyes, and then it was gone. She reached behind my head, pulling me to her, and our lips met with startling ferocity, mouth pressing hard on mouth, tongue finding tongue. She bit my lip and I tasted blood, neither of us pulling away.

I drew her closer to me, her spine curving until I thought it would snap, then I pushed her away roughly and we stood apart, staring at one another like adversaries about to fight till death. She smiled and drew her tongue across her lips. Lips that were stained crimson with my blood.

She removed her shirt and then, reaching round her back, unzipped her skirt and let it fall to the floor, standing there half-naked and vulnerable. I gasped when I saw her bruised body, so perfect in its form. She walked across to me and pulled at my t-shirt. I grabbed her arm and she winced, bringing her hand down hard across my face, catching my already damaged lip. The pain felt good and I tore off my t-shirt, breathless and with my heart racing. Rachel reached for my zip, freeing me of my cargos and I reached behind her back, unclasping her bra. I pulled her into me, grabbing her hair as I did so. Her head snapped back and I drew a line with my tongue across her exposed throat, breathing hot down her neck. She gasped and I nibbled at her earlobe, increasing the pressure until she almost squealed with pleasure.

Suddenly she drew her legs around my waist, biting down gently on my shoulder and neck, her fingernails digging into the flesh of my back. I carried Rachel across to the sofa, throwing her down and falling hard on top of her. She lay back into the cushions, legs still wrapped around my waist. We kissed again, this time with less force, a teasing kind of kiss, tongues meeting lightly at their tips before drawing back; she found the split in my lip and tenderly kissed it.

I pulled back and looked at her, taking in her beauty, her vulnerability. She bit her lip seductively, hooking her thumbs around the lacy band of her knickers and lowering them teasingly. I gently kissed her neck, my hand cupping her breast, finding her nipple, my fingers pinching until it stood hard and proud from its fleshy mound. She moaned, her eyes were half closed, lips apart. Her hand reached down and grabbed me, squeezing hard and I winced. I took her nipple between my teeth and bit down. She cried out, gripping me tighter, her hand sliding along my length, trying to force me into her. Not yet I smiled, my tip stroking her teasingly before pulling back further. I ran my tongue across her smooth flat stomach, making my way south. She groaned as I avoided her lady garden, instead running the tip of my tongue down her inner thigh.

'Aaahh!' she cried, as the tip of my hot tongue found her, surprising her with its hurried ferocity. I slowly formed a figure eight on her burning flesh, before finding her love bud and attacking it with short sharp jabs, my teeth lightly grazing her soft skin. She squirmed beneath me.

'Please Jared,' she begged breathlessly. 'Please.'

I took her swiftly, taking her breath away, unable to hold back any longer, withdrawing slowly before deeply penetrating her again and again. Inside she was hot and wet and I could feel my own heat rising, drawing from the very core of me. Her sighs escalated, turning to squeals, increasing in both length and frequency.

Her toes curled, digging into the sofa, her back arching, pulling me in deeper, her thighs opened wider so as to offer no resistance. She offered herself fully and I took her, her squeals becoming whimpers, a lone tear rolling down her cheek. I withdrew fully, then plunged into her hard with a cry of pleasure, and as our juices mingled, all of my pent up feelings and emotions of the last few months were released. Our bodies shuddered and sent spasms of pleasure riding through us like waves, gradually subsiding as we held each other and kissed softly, lightly, our drenched bodies cocooned in the afterglow.

We moved to the bedroom and made love twice more that night. The hunger had gone, to be replaced by tenderness and longing, and when we had finished, we held each other, Rachel softly weeping until we fell into an exhausted, dreamless sleep.

When I awoke, she was gone.

The only reminder of her, a drop of blood on the pillow and a crumpled sheet, bleached white in the moonlight through the open curtains.

Chapter Thirty Seven

A Dream Within A Dream

I followed the trail of blood down the deserted street. I was out, alone in the middle of the street, and yet I felt fine. No narrowing vista, no swimming horizons, heartbeat and breathing regular. I felt fine, even following a trail of blood.

I knew I was meant to meet someone; it was like a scene from a Vettriano painting.

I was to meet the man inside one of those all night diners, like the ones they have in American film noir. Although there was an air of menace about the scene, I knew it wasn't related to the man.

I stepped inside the diner and the heavens opened behind me. The place was empty, but for one man sat at the bar with his back to me. I ordered coffee and walked towards him. He seemed reassuringly familiar. He was a tall, big-boned man. Well dressed in an expensive overcoat, beneath his fedora his hair was the darker side of grey. My excitement grew when I realised I was to meet Leonard Cohen.

'I took pills for my memory,' Leonard Cohen told me. 'But I could not stop it from erasing… I had a family once.'

Just as he started to turn toward me, the scene changed. I was still in the bar, but I was alone. Even the waitress had gone; only a steaming cup of coffee on the counter remained from the previous scene.

'It's going to happen very soon...' came Cohen's disembodied voice. 'The great event that will end the horror.'

I was suddenly aware of being watched. From across the road, beneath a lamppost in the pouring rain stood the boy, Zachary. Somehow he seemed different, familiar but different. Suddenly, I knew beyond all doubt that this was not a real lad, but the spirit of a lad, and I wasn't afraid of him anymore. On seeing me turn, he started to run and all at once in need of answers, I ran out into the night after him.

We were in real Bogart territory now. Not Bogart the lover, Bogart the villain. The streets were dark and still and silent. But for the dripping and gushing of rainwater in the gutters it was quiet, unnaturally so. I followed the boy for miles or so it seemed, never once troubled by the pouring rain, never once made breathless by the exertion of running. In the distance I could see flashing lights, and the boy ran towards these, up toward the river.

Close up I could see a police cordon. A small crowd was gathering. Stood apart from the crowd were two ladies, sheltering beneath a large umbrella. They were dressed in clothes from the thirties or forties, although they seemed quite young. I slowed down and as I passed them, they lifted the umbrella to look at me.
As the sombre glow of the streetlight penetrated the shadows beneath the umbrella, I turned to glance at them. Strangely one resembled Beth, the way she was the night I

met her, all those years ago at a college party. The other looked like a younger version of Clara. This one whispered something to her friend and they both laughed. I turned away. feeling uncomfortable.

When I reached the river, the boy had gone and I made my way toward the crowd of people, who moved aside to let me through. There, on the road beside the river, lay the dripping carcass of a young woman who had been dragged from the water. She was naked, white as a pearl. Her river-darkened hair splayed about her head. In the moonlight there glistened a jagged-edged silver blade, which protruded from just beneath her ribcage.

With horror I looked into the cold, lifeless eyes of Rachel.

Chapter Thirty Eight

Graham

Graham sat alone in the restaurant. It was early. He was nervous.

He had been to the barber's and wore his best suit. It smelled a little of mothballs. His mother had put it away in a box after his father's funeral. It had been a little crumpled but he'd managed to iron most of the creases out. He wore a half dead carnation in his buttonhole and nervously kept blowing into his hands to check the freshness of his breath. He nursed a small Coke with no ice, and on the table in front of him lay a single red rose.

He could scarcely believe his luck! That very morning he had plucked up enough courage to ask Lisa out for dinner and she had said yes. At first he had suggested going over to hers, but she seemed uncomfortable with the idea and had recommended they go to her favourite restaurant instead. It was a little pricey, but she was well worth it. He recalled how she'd blushed before accepting to go out on a date with him. She was a true lady alright, and even the giggles and whispers of their colleagues who had obviously heard, had failed to dampen his mood.

His nerves were mounting as the time of their meeting neared. He picked up his drink and then put it down again.

He checked his nails and viewed himself in the back of a spoon before blowing on it and polishing it with his napkin.

He glanced at his watch. It was five minutes past seven-thirty, the arranged meeting time. He tried to combat his irritation by telling himself that some things were worth waiting for, but made a mental note to talk to her about her punctuality, should she want a long-term relationship to develop. He was beginning to sweat and he wiped away the beads of perspiration from his forehead with his napkin. He had been there over half an hour now; the waiter hovered anxiously, and the elderly couple at the next table had begun to stare.

By almost eight, his stomach was in knots and his throat felt dry and constricted. The waiter looked at him questioningly. Graham knew he only had an allotted time slot for the table and he gestured five more minutes to the man.

He subconsciously stroked the silky, scented petals of the rose and it felt good between his fingers. Beautiful, untainted, fragile...*snap!* The head of the rose came away in his hand, but still his onslaught continued, tearing it apart, the leaves falling like wounded, battle-weary soldiers, the petals blood red against the crisp, white tablecloth.

He could feel a set of eyes on him, but not from the people in the restaurant who had already looked away in embarrassment, clearly feeling uncomfortable. Not by his obvious despair at having been let down by someone, but by his growing anger and his seemingly deranged conduct.

Graham's face was the colour of the rose petals as he turned slowly towards the restaurant's huge picture window. There, with their faces pressed against the glass, pointing at him and laughing, stood the vast majority of his colleagues from the office. He could even make out one or two members of senior management.

He felt the colour drain from his face. It had been a set up! A cruel joke, right from the start. Tears of frustration, self-pity and rage stung his eyes. He struggled for breath and fell to the floor clutching his chest. The waiter and what looked like the restaurant manager came over to help him to his feet, and he pushed them away roughly.

The lady at the nearest table shook her head with disbelief. Graham threw a crumpled note on the table for the drink and stormed towards the door, knocking the table with his hip as he did so.

A single red petal dropped to the floor and was crushed underfoot by the waiter.

Outside the pavement was clear. His tormentors were thankfully gone and the high road was unusually tranquil for the time of night. He rushed to his car and slammed the door. He sat inside, gasping for breath, his head buried in his hands until long after his sobs had subsided. Eventually, even his whimpers died down. After what seemed like hours of sitting in silence, he put the key into the ignition and pulled away. Avoiding turning left into the main road that led out of town and towards Burlington Road, he swing the car right and onto the A road that led towards the town centre and Lisa's flat.

Chapter Thirty Nine

I awoke to see a face close to mine and looked straight into a pair of large yellow eyes, and I knew that unless Rachel had grown a grey beard and developed halitosis while we slept, it was Bogart eye-balling me until I got up and made his breakfast. I groaned and rolled over, but he wasn't to be put off and began rubbing the back of my head with his face, tapping my shoulder with his paw and purring loudly in my ear. My head was heavy with all the gin from the previous night, and I groaned again as I turned to face him.

'This could be the end of a beautiful friendship, Humph,' I warned him, and in true Bogart style he punched me in the eye. I sighed and got up, rubbing my aching head. I picked up my robe from the floor and followed him downstairs.

My clothes, the two glasses and the empty bottle of gin littered the lounge where Rachel and I had left them when we ran upstairs to bed. I yawned and walked down the hallway and towards the kitchen to feed the cat, scratching my stubbly chin and wondering why Rachel had left before dawn, when I stopped at the kitchen door and gasped at the sight that greeted me.

Beth was sitting at the kitchen table just as Rachel had only last night, with Bogart on her lap. Her face was grim as she sat nursing a cold cup of tea, and screwed up in her left hand was a note left for me by Rachel.

'Hello, Jared,' Beth said coldly. Bogart, detecting her mood, slipped off her knee and came rubbing around my ankles. I ignored her. Inwardly I felt angry that she'd seen me like this, dishevelled and hung over. I knew I was living up to her expectations of me.

I went over and filled the kettle before pouring Bogart's food into his bowl. He sniffed at it in disgust and then high-tailed it out of the cat flap, off to Clara, who I know feeds him tinned tuna, but not before shooting me a meaningful glance as if to say 'Good luck pal.'

I poured myself a coffee and then made for the lounge, throwing myself on the sofa and stretching out. I thought momentarily of Rachel and hoped she was ok. The thought left me feeling guilty, and I hated myself for feeling that way. Beth sighed from the kitchen and followed me in; she sat on the seat opposite and watched as I sipped my coffee. I felt uncomfortable under her steady, unfaltering gaze and hoped it didn't show.

I noticed with some satisfaction that she looked tired. She still looked good, boy did she look good in her cropped leather biker and long, tight black skirt, but there were dark circle beneath her eyes, indicative of many sleepless nights, and she looked pale and drawn.

'What do you want, Bethan?' I sighed impatiently.

My heart was racing and I was beginning to feel sick, but I noticed her wince at the use of her formal name, a name used by her father and only when she was in trouble, and that gave me some leverage.

'I see it didn't take you long to replace me,' she said. She skims Rachel's folded note across the coffee table to me. It fell to the floor before reaching me, and I let it lie on the rug, like a gauntlet thrown between us. I swung my legs around and sat up straight, glaring at Beth.

'What do you want?' I repeated. I knew perfectly well what she wanted; tears, recriminations, me begging, pleading with her to stay and promising to change, to make things work between us. All she got was a cold, hard stare.

I noticed a look of what? Uncertainty? Alarm? In those cat-like eyes of hers, and she looked for a second as if she was going to cry. Then her features hardened.

'My solicitor tells me you haven't been answering his mail.'

'Is that what the letters were?' I smirked. 'I filed them in the bin.'

She lowered her head, her curls falling on her face. Her hair had grown since we last saw each other. It suited her.

'I want a divorce,' she said, pushing her hair back out of her eyes.

I felt as though my insides had been ripped out. I'd known it was coming, but somehow hearing it in words from Beth's own lips made it final, inevitable.

'So,' I said. 'You leave me without a word of warning. I hear nothing from you for over six months and now you're back and making demands.' My eyes were blazing. I could feel all the anger I'd suppressed over the last six months welling up inside. I fought hard to keep it in check.

'Jared, it's over. There's no going back.' She looked a little nervous.

'Going back!' I spat the words out. '*Going back!* You think I want to go back?' I laughed with incredulity. 'I *hate* you for what you did... Do you have the papers here? I'll sign them now.'

She looked shocked and hurt by my outburst. I'd never raised my voice to her before. Her lip began to tremble.

'You, you don't understand, Jared. I had to go. I did... I did something terrible, something unforgivable.'

I looked at her and frowned. I had no idea of what she meant. What could she have done that was so bad she had to leave?

Beth started to sob. I hated seeing her like that, but when I reached out to her, she pulled away, and suddenly I felt hurt and rejected.

'I, I...Jared, I killed our baby. I had an abortion without you knowing, and now...and now I'd do anything to go back and undo it, but I can't, Jared, I can't and I'm so, so sorry.'

I couldn't breathe and I felt sick, like my heart had been ripped out. Beth reached into her handbag and brought out a tissue. I watched her as she dried her eyes and attempted to pull herself back together, but I couldn't find anything to say. Beth pregnant! Our baby aborted! The words reverberated around my skull. Why did she tell me this? I didn't want to know this. How was I supposed to feel? I leaned back against the cushions of the sofa, tucking my knees up against my chin in a foetal position.

'I'm sorry,' she said, standing and straightening her skirt. 'Could I use your bathroom?'

Your bathroom. At that point, I realised she'd moved out mentally, as well as physically. She no longer felt at home here. I closed down then, pushing any feelings I might have had to the back in my mind so I didn't have to deal with them.

'You know the way,' I replied coolly. I watched her as she made her way to the bathroom, taking in all the changes I had made to the house. She returned composed and sat, and we stared at each other in silence.

'Why now, Beth? Why did you feel the need to tell me this?'

'I…I needed to tell someone. I had to speak to *someone.*'

'So feel free to unburden yourself on *me,*' I said, the contempt evident in my voice.

'It was your child,' she retorted, blinking back the tears.

'No,' I sighed, weary with the conversation. 'It was a fertilised egg that you chose to flush down the toilet without telling me.' I looked at her coldly. 'It would have been my child, our child, but you decided to make that decision for me, without me.'

She stared at me in shock. 'Jared, what have you become?' she whispered.

'What you made me,' I said. 'Just what you made me.'

I looked at her but she couldn't meet my eyes, and she fidgeted with the buttons on her shirt before picking up her handbag from the table.

'I'll be taking Bogart with me.' She sniffed. 'If you could get his things together and help me to the car…'

'I'll see you hanged first,' I hissed at her, surprised by my own venom, and she stared at me. She looked ugly. Her red, crumpled face was distorted into a mask of shock and despair. She seemed somehow ridiculous and small, and I suddenly realised that I didn't love her anymore.

She reached into her handbag and pulled out a letter. 'Ok,' she said, standing and adjusting the purse strap on her shoulder. 'If you could please sign this. It's addressed to my solicitor…'

She held the letter out to me, but I just looked at her without emotion. She dropped it on the table and hesitated before walking towards the door. I didn't attempt to stop her, nor did I speak or acknowledge that she was leaving. She turned to look at me one last time and then she was gone.

I didn't move for a long time afterwards, not even when Bogart settled himself on my knee. The shadows lengthened and evening gathered, turning everything from murky grey to almost impenetrable black, and still I didn't move.

I merely sat staring at the space she'd occupied.

Chapter Forty

Clara

Breaking her father's heart was the one thing Clara couldn't live with. Her mother's ranting, her sister's 'I told you so's' were water off a duck's back to Clara. But her poor old dad's disappointed face was more than she could bear.

'I think you'd better leave,' her mother had told her.

After staying at her friend's for a while, Clara moved into a small flat above a chemist shop and took a job in a baker's until the baby was born. The baker had been a friend of her father's, and although money was tight, she had been content to live that way for a while. She still missed the stage, but her engorged stomach and the little kicks she felt whenever she sang to it reminded her that she had more important things to think about now.

She gave birth to a son and named him Michael. She doted on the boy, men and socialising taking a back seat until Michael was four, when she was introduced to a lovely man named Ted Morris. Almost twenty years her senior, Ted was a client at the bakers where Clara now worked in the office.

She knew he loved her right from the start, and although she was never to be *in* love with him, she grew to love Ted almost as much as she loved her son. In marrying Ted she had been reunited with her estranged family, and when her dad told her as he led her down the aisle that she had made him proud, she had cried tears of joy.

Ted moved his new family into Burlington Road, and Clara settled into domestic bliss, never once thinking of the stage or the cut-throat world of show business. Her husband never questioned her about Michael's father and the boy, now five, grew up believing Ted was his dad. Much to the annoyance of Clara's sister, he became the apple of his granddad's eye too.

Only years later, after Ted had been cruelly cut down by cancer and Michael had moved away to university, did Clara start feeling sad and alone. She was thinking about the life she could have had on stage and screen. She'd had the talent, the looks and everything else she needed to have lived the dream, but she had been a foolish girl, charmed and seduced by a life as celluloid and false as the images on a movie screen.

Clara sat on her bed, surrounded by mementos and knick-knacks. Treasured objects and treasured memories. She looked at Michael's photo and thought of how much he resembled her father, rather than his own. She had never told him about his own father, whose career had been cut short after he was accused of raping a young actress, whom he had starred with. A bitter divorce amid tales of spousal abuse and homosexual affairs had been the final nail in his professional coffin. She had heard of his death recently and felt only the tiniest pang of remorse at the news.

Her own wedding photo caught her eye. How happy she'd looked, how charming Ted had been and how lucky she had been to have him. Hers was a good life; she had no cause to complain. Soon she would leave her home on Burlington Road and start a new life elsewhere, far from these long, lonely nights and dusty, silent rooms. Despite feeling sad about the things she'd be leaving behind Clara knew there was room in her suitcase for the things she treasured most, just as there was room in heart for her memories.

Chapter Forty One

After Beth left for a second time, several things happened at once.

Following our one night together, Rachel disappeared. It wasn't that I wanted a replay particularly, although it wouldn't have been entirely unwelcome, but I was concerned for her. I watched from my landing window, hoping she would come out into the garden, but all was still from Chez Joaquin. The boy, Tris, it seemed, had also gone.

All was ominously quiet, and as darkness fell on Burlington Road, I saw strange figures lurking around outside. They appeared to be in costume and it seemed they were going from door to door. My heart leapt into my mouth as a sudden sharp tap on my door made me jump away from the window. I made my way nervously down the stairs and along the hallway.

'Trick or treat,' called out a voice from behind the door. I almost cried out with relief. Of course, it was October thirty-first! All Hallow's Eve. I suddenly felt silly and was about to open the door when I remembered I had nothing for them. Beth always bought a big bag of sweets for the kids, but I hadn't even realised what day it was. Not that I was up to seeing them anyway.

I slunk off to the darkened lounge and hid until they went away. I felt bad. I felt foolish and I wondered what the neighbours thought of me. Not that there seemed to be anyone around to notice. Rachel had gone and Simeon seemed to be keeping a low profile, not that we saw him much anyway, and I remembered overhearing that the Meldrew's were off to a wedding in Yorkshire that weekend, so I presumed they'd already left.

Nothing to report from over at Graham's either. Although I had heard Margaret Meldrew saying, just before they set off, how his mother had been taken into a nursing home following a fall that had broken her hip. Hmm! I had my suspicions.

My concerns for Clara had deepened too, after seeing two official-looking guys going into her house that morning. If only I could have nipped across and saw how she was.

With little or no signs of life on Burlington Road, the witches, zombies and monsters having left for a more profitable area, I felt isolated and alone. The silence was almost creepy, and the only other presence I could feel was that of the boy standing and watching from beneath the lamppost across the road.

Once again I felt as if the walls were closing in. I felt suffocated and opened the back doors, the cold, autumn air came rushing through and I took a deep breath. Looking out onto the garden through the void, I rapidly felt exposed and anxious.

A sudden movement among the shadows down by the shed startled me. I knew it was just an animal. It could even have been Bogart, but I felt nervy and slightly nauseous.

I lay down on the floor and breathed deeply, my nerves soon steadying themselves. I knew this couldn't continue for much longer. I would have to do something about it. I felt cowardly and ashamed, hiding indoors like this.

I had tried to go out again after Beth's visit. Only to the garden, but I'd felt so anxious, so dizzy, that I was almost sick. I cried out with frustration. It seemed I was to spend the rest of my life indoors and I couldn't bear the thought of that.

Bogart had watched me from the lawn and I wondered again as to whether or not he thought I was a full cat biscuit. It was hard to describe the way I was feeling at that moment. I'd been starting to feel a little better before Beth's visit. A little more connected, not so alone. After, I felt estranged not only from her, but from the outside world, not an entirely alien feeling admittedly but that time it was different. I think Beth's visit had brought with it some closure. I no longer wondered where she was, or why she went. I wasn't sure I really missed her anymore. I was neither left in the dark nor left hoping, and I did want that divorce. I felt I needed it to move on.

After the visit, I called my solicitor and explained all to him. I signed the divorce papers (Beth, it seemed, was stating irreconcilable differences.) and he sent out his clerk to collect them. I felt strangely relieved when I signed for him to begin proceedings.

I had been thinking long and hard about Beth's deceit. I wasn't angry with her, more saddened and disgusted by her. But for the times we'd had together and the love we'd shared, I would try hard, *very hard*, to forgive her, even though it was those very things that made such treachery so unforgivable.

I was tired and depressed and about to go off to bed early when a loud knock on the door interrupted me. I thought of ignoring it, assuming it was another kid playing trick or treat, and then my brother Nathan shouted to me. Armed with beer, pizza and computer games, he was a sight for sore eyes. I could have hugged him. He stayed until late and although we were not really heart to heart type siblings, I told him all about Beth and the divorce, and I felt better for unburdening myself. I knew that anything told to Nathan would not go any further, and I felt a step closer to humanity once more.

Chapter Forty Two

Alan

You received a letter from Joaquin. You recognised his spidery handwriting on the envelope. Letters are such rare things these days, you tell yourself. Yours lies unopened on the table in the hallway, beside the lamp your mother bought from Tiffany's.

The headaches are getting worse, the painkillers doing little to prevent it.

'Like an aspirin for a severed limb' you tell the man in your shaving mirror. You stopped shaving ages ago. You only look at it now for the company.

Your life plays itself back to you in dreams. A Pathe newsreel of images portraying memories and regrets, of chances missed, of mistakes revisited. Of time wasted and of innocence lost. You watch it unfold with weary resignation, alone between sweat-drenched sheets.

Sometimes you dream you are on a train. The old fashioned kind. You are alone in your compartment. Steaming through the night, travelling through time. Each station a different era. Another stage in your life. Scenes flash by, some sepia-tinted like a fading memory. Others, rich in glorious Technicolour.

A quiet, bookish boy stands ashen-faced between a doting mother and an indifferent father, as they pose for a family photograph. Later, that same mother sheds hitherto unseen tears for unborn grand-children she will never hold, before being stricken by a debilitating illness that would claim her life. Your father, whom you adored but could never get close to, himself dying of a broken heart less than six months later. The guilt at finding your mother annoying and clingy despite your love for her haunts you still.

You watch yourself, the angst-ridden teen, raging against conflicting emotions, disgusted by your thoughts and feelings towards other men. Then as a student, experimental, sexually promiscuous, but still disgusted, un-accepting of your needs and desires. Relationships you found unfulfilling and superficial. Lovers who came and went.

Your professional life was one of handicaps, birdies and the old boy network, your colleagues believing you to be widowed, or like so many 'married to the job.'

In confessing the love you felt for a straight man, you laid your soul bare and in doing so lost a wonderful friend. But in accepting your inevitable death, after years of self-conflict you finally accept yourself for who you are.

Chapter Forty Three

I found myself missing my neighbours and their comings and goings. Still, Burlington Road was portentously quiet. The Meldrews were undoubtedly taking in the delights of God's own county before they got back. Their neatly trimmed hedges seemed to have grown in their absence. Not much, just enough to block the view of Rachel's drive from my hallway window.

Still no signs of Rachel or her son, but I'd spotted Simeon's BMW a couple of times parked outside of the Meldrew's. I'd even seen him with someone who I assumed to be his mistress. A six-foot blonde in head to toe Jaeger. The guy's got some balls, I gave him that.

Sylvia called around with what looked like a casserole in her hand and I hid behind the curtain and watched. Although we were never really that close (I always found her too over-bearing), it occurred to me how distant I'd become from her. What was more disconcerting was the fact that I didn't care.

I saw another man going into Clara's house and my imagination was in overdrive. Later I saw Clara coming out and getting into a car with him. I wondered she was up to.

Of Graham, I had seen precious little. In fact, I probably hadn't seen him for a week or so. His car was still in the drive, but the house remained dark and silent. Maybe he was away, enjoying his new-found freedom with the old girl finally off his hands, although it seemed out of character.

About the others on the street, (and there weren't that many, it only being a little avenue), I knew precious little. People came and went regularly from number forty. They didn't seem to stay long and kept themselves to themselves. It was a strange house, that one. I sometimes felt as though there were invisible eyes watching from behind the curtains. I pacified myself by saying it was all in my mind and cursed my active imagination and overwrought nerves.

Ours was once a friendly neighbourhood, but with young professionals moving in, after being driven out of the city by sky-high housing costs, the rapidly changing face of suburbia meant close-knit communities were a thing of the past. Ergo, apart from the nosey Meldrews, the only person taking an interest in the lives, deaths and misdemeanours of his immediate neighbours was a lonely no-lifer like me, confined to his house and filling his endless waking hours with speculative musings about the lives of others. It was a sad existence, definitely not one to be recommended, and how long I personally could sustain this desperately lonely existence was another matter entirely.

Chapter Forty Four

Joaquin

The airport was hot and crowded, surprisingly so as this was not the holiday season. Joaquin had missed the flight to Gatwick, and unless he wanted to fly out to Manchester and then take the train, he had a long wait for the next plane.

Something told him he had to get home to Burlington to see Alan. What he didn't understand was the urgency.

He would text Jared when he arrived in England, but he'd already decided to stay in town. He knew his friend would want him to stay over, but he felt at such short notice that it would be an imposition.

He sat down on one of the benches in the terminal and tried to get comfortable.

The flight information board was notifying of cancellations and delays to the schedule, and he groaned aloud when he saw that his flight was to be one of the casualties. He dragged himself off the bench and over to one of the airport's bustling bars. Although food was the last thing on his mind, it would pass the time, and he didn't relish the long wait.

Chapter Forty Five

Graham

Graham watched Lisa swim from the depths of her drug-induced stupor to consciousness. He thought of offering her water, but as she couldn't raise her head yet he waited, leaning back in his chair, his emotions toward her swinging from tenderness to hatred.

Graham hadn't gone straight to Lisa's after the restaurant. Instead, he had turned off into a quiet lay-by beside the Total garage, on the road that led up toward the recreational ground.

He had taken a petrol can from the back of his car and from it had filled a glass bottle, which he kept in the car for emergencies. He stuffed the top of the bottle with a rag which he used for his mirrors and windscreen.

It always helped to be prepared. His father, a Boy Scout leader, had taught him that, and although Graham knew he'd been a bitter disappointment to the man, he had always abided by his father's strict disciplines.

He had put the bottle into his briefcase, careful not to spill its volatile contents in the car and with his matches, another survival essential, in his jacket pocket, he had driven the half a mile or so to the offices of Barton, Withnall & Reeve in the middle of town. There, he had calmly walked through reception, bidding good evening to the security guard there, after flashing the ID badge he always kept in his wallet. He had taken the lift to the second floor, typed in the code to his office door, removed a huge pile of paperwork from the desks and littered the floor with it. Then without a second thought, he lit the Molotov and threw it against the far wall.

Graham stood for a moment or two and watched the fire take hold, quickly sweeping across the floor like a burning oil slick on a calm lake, consuming everything in its path.
He knew that within five minutes the smoke would have reached the motion detectors and the alarm would be set off, alerting the security guard on the desk in the foyer.
He also knew that by the time the emergency services had made their way through from the next big town, it would already be too late for the offices of Bastard, Wanker and Rats-arse.

He stood a minute more, hypnotised by the fire, his insane mask of hatred made all the more sinister in the shadows by the rigid grin and the flames that danced wretchedly in those wild, deranged eyes.

Lisa suddenly groaned and her eyes flickered open. The room was dark but a chink of light shone through a small cracked window, where dust motes danced and twirled in the spotlight. Graham yanked off the tape that covered her mouth, and she screamed when his leering face appeared in front of her.

'Shut up you nasty little bitch,' he snarled, soaking a cloth and covering her nose and mouth.

He pulled the chair up in front of her and replaced the tape over her mouth, watching as she slowly slipped away into oblivion.

He had sat in the car for a good while outside Lisa's flat, waiting for one of the other tenants to come back home and open the front door. He felt surprisingly calm as he waited, the music on the radio doing its job well in satisfying his jangling nerves. But Graham wasn't acting on nerves. Fuelled by hatred for himself, his life and those around him, Graham had reached breaking point and now someone had to pay.

He looked up at Lisa's window, a look of pure hatred casting its shadow across his face.

'I thought you were different,' he said. His eyes misted over and he wiped them on his jacket sleeve. Mustn't cry, he slated himself. A man must never show weakness.

He saw the faces of his colleagues, floating before his eyes. He heard their laughter. They were pointing at him. They had tried to publicly ridicule him and now they would pay the price. Or at least, one of them would.

His anger was rising again and he thumped the steering wheel with the heel of his fist. He thought he could hear sirens, their wail muted by the distance. He felt strangely soothed by the sound; soon his revenge would be complete.

In retrospect, he felt certain Lisa had been coerced in what had taken place tonight. He was sure she had been genuine and that her feelings for him were as real as his were for her. But if she didn't love him now, he was determined that she would come to do so in time, away from the poisonous influence of the office.

A sudden movement made him look up, and he saw a young couple making their way up the path. With a steady manner that belied his intentions, Graham slipped out of the car and calmly followed them. The young woman looked a little surprised, but he was a smartly dressed, middle aged gentleman, so she held the door for him nonetheless.

'Thank you, dear' he said, smiling sweetly. He could feel her eyes on him as he walked up the stairs to Lisa's flat.

When he reached Lisa's front door, he stopped and took a deep breath. He stood with his back tight to the wall. What was he doing? This is madness, he told himself. He wasn't a bad man. Not a bad man really. He'd been pushed too far, that was all. It wasn't too late; no damage had been done really. He could simply go away. His mother would be taken care of now; he could just disappear, like the Fitzpatrick boy from across the road.

He heard Lisa laughing from inside, a raucous, mocking laugh. His face darkened and his cold, steely eyes glinted dangerously.

'Coward,' he hissed at himself. 'Always the coward. Will you keep on running for the rest of your life?'

Lisa was still laughing when she opened the door. The smile drained away from her face when she saw who stood outside.

'Why would you do that Lisa?' he asked when she next roused. 'What did I ever do to you but admire you?'

Lisa mumbled incoherently behind the tape.

'I can remove the tape Lisa,' Graham said. 'But you need to promise not to scream. Screaming will get right on my nerves and I need to be calm. *You need me to be calm.*'

Lisa's muffled reply implied that she would not scream, and Graham removed the gag.

'Please,' she begged. 'Please, Graham, let me go!'

Chapter Forty Six

Looking over at number forty that morning I shuddered. It had always been a creepy, desolate place. Your classic Hammer house, it had always fired my imagination, but lately, though, I was certain I'd seen movement among the shadows.

Alan, who had lived on the street forever, once told me that the old guy who owned the place had been good friends with Graham's parents, so he had doubtless given them a key to look after the house in his absence. Probably, what I thought I'd seen was nothing more than Graham doing just that.

I could well imagine him stalking through the darkened rooms, looking for signs of intruders and hoping beyond hope to corner some young lad who'd broken in for a dare. I didn't quite know what it was, but I thought there was something really wrong about that guy.

I was feeling a little happier. Joaquin had sent me a text message. He was coming home any day soon and he would be around for a while. At least until he'd earned his next fare. I was a little bemused and upset by his refusal of my offer of a place to stay, choosing instead to stay in a bedsit in town. Still, my dearest friend was coming back and it might just give me the impetus I needed to get my own life back on track.

Beth also sent me a text message. She'd been given the opportunity to stay with an old college friend in New Zealand for a while and she'd made a snap decision to go. She asked me to have her things ready. She would send a man with a van to pick it all up and it would be taken into storage for the time being. Thankfully, I'd packed it all away in the spare room, although I didn't relish the moment when all of her belongings were gone and the finality of it hit home as it inevitably would.

I'd been dreaming for the past few nights about the child she'd aborted and kept hearing, or imagined I kept hearing, a baby crying. It would wake me in the cool, stillness of the morning, the piteous wail of the newborn abandoned in its cot, calling for a mother that would never come. Once or twice I got up out of bed and scanned the empty, twilit street.

'Bloody cats,' I said to Bogart, who observed me contemptuously, with one eye closed as though my actions didn't warrant the use of both.

In the dream, I was watching the ghost of the boy beneath the lamppost across the street. Bizarrely, he never looked the same age when I saw him. Now fourteen, now about ten, but always watching me and with the same mournful expression, as if he was lost and looking for something he'd perhaps never known, but knew existed. What he wanted with me, the boy Zachary, I could not imagine, but there was a familiarity about him that I couldn't quite put my finger on. Maybe he'd found me in the darkness. Maybe he saw in me a kindred spirit, another lost soul.

I was called from watching the boy by Beth, who sleepily asked me to check on the baby. Sometimes the child was dead when I got there. His face purple, his sightless eyes staring straight ahead. Other times, I looked into the cot and he was gurgling and laughing, despite the urgent wailing that drew me to him. He was laid on his stomach in this dream and his head turned at an unnatural angle to look at me. Sometimes he had my face, an adult's face and other times, he had no face at all. Like my Grandma in previous dreams. The faceless or dead baby dream should have really unnerved me the most, but it was the dream with the baby with an adult face that I found the creepiest.

I was in the spare room gathering up my soon-to-be ex-wife's possessions. They were for the most part boxed up, but a few bits and pieces I hadn't been able to find room for were lying scattered around. I found a book of poetry she'd written at university, and although I never really appreciated poetry, I had to admit some of them were very good. I also found a dog-eared copy of 'The Bell Jar' by Sylvia Plath. On the inside leaf she'd written; 'this book belongs to Mrs. Beth Colne,' with the name crossed out and re-written several times, as though she were practising her signature for when we were married. It made me smile. We weren't even engaged at that time and it seemed uncharacteristically girly for her, or maybe I never really knew Beth at all?

I found some old CD singles, Suede and Happy Mondays, and photos of the two of us taken over ten years ago. I looked gangly and goofy with my messy student hairdo, but Beth looked beautiful, young and carefree. In another, we were arm in arm. There were several of us in the picture, all friends, but Beth and I gazed into each other's eyes as though there were not another living soul around.

I was suddenly overcome with a feeling of melancholy for my halcyon days. I did know her back then, I was sure of it. As I threw the pictures into a box, I wondered why she'd changed so much and what the future had in store for us now.

I was almost done and about to start carrying the boxes downstairs when I heard a shuffling noise coming from a large tea chest at the back of the room. I hoped it wasn't a rat, because if it was, it was a bloody big one, and Bogart the hunter was nowhere to be seen.

I approached with caution. I didn't fancy cornering a big rat. I shuddered as I heard the noise again; a definite scratching sound, coming from inside the chest. With one foot raised, I gently knocked the box onto its side, spilling its contents onto the floor. It was devoid of life and there was nothing there I could see that would have made such a noise.

I was about to throw everything back in when I spotted an old VHS tape on the floor. What's odd is I don't remember it being there when I packed. I'm sure I'd have noticed an antique like that. I picked it up and read the label on the side. Written in my ex-wife's elaborate hand, it said 'Beth's bridal shower, August twenty-four.' The rest was illegible.

We'd bought a DVD/VHS player way back, as Beth had inherited a lot of old black & white films from her aunt. I slid the tape into the machine and waited for it to load.

It was for the most part what I'd expected, a lot of silly, drunken girls, a lot of games and a lot of giggling. I couldn't believe some of the things they talked about, I hadn't realised girls could be so crude. I found myself at the butt of most of their jokes, with Beth defending me to the hilt and receiving more that her fair share of light-hearted teasing for her trouble. I rolled the tape on and found the girls even more drunk. A couple of them had shoved a cushion up the front of Beth's dress and she'd flopped down hard on the sofa, rubbing her 'bump' as though exhausted.

'Awww,' one of the girls mocked, patting the bump. 'Boy or girl?'

Another girl laughed. 'And what will Mr. and Mrs. Colne call their firstborn?' There was a long wait, some static and then the film froze. But when I finally heard Beth's answer, it chilled me to the bone.

'Our first, last and only child will be a boy, and we shall call him Zachary Edward Colne.'

Chapter Forty Seven

The Meldrews

They drove home in silence, only the sound of the rain on the car roof and the nervous yapping of the dogs breaking the monotony.

Jeremy had all but given up trying to converse with his wife. Any attempts so do had been met with half-hearted, monosyllabic answers, and anyway, with a storm brewing and him towing, he needed to concentrate all of his efforts on the road. He had grown used to Margaret's moods over the years and he refused to pander to them. After all, hadn't they just had a lovely few days away? Well, he'd enjoyed it anyway. Let the silly cow sulk.

They'd met at a dance thirty-five years ago, when he was an apprentice electrical engineer and she was in secretarial college. She'd been quite a looker back then, Margaret. All of the lads had fancied her, and he could never quite understand why she'd chosen him. Still, he was well on his way to being qualified and in time his earnings would be quite substantial. Besides, he thought cynically, he'd been the only one with a car.

He remembered his first car and smiled. An Mk2 Ford Zephyr it was, two-tone blue. All chrome and tailfins. He'd had some fun in that car before he'd tied the knot. He'd had some fun in that car with Margaret, too. He looked at her profile in the mirror, as she stared passively out of the window. She still was an attractive woman, he mused.

A sudden gush of rain hit the window and the caravan rocked unsteadily in the wind. His wife turned and looked at him nervously.

'Be home soon, dear.' He smiled reassuringly.

Chapter Forty Eight

The storm began around two. It had been unseasonably warm for the past two days, but the house had remained cold. That day there was a distinct chill about the place, and I made a mental note to call the plumber to take a look at the heating.

It had been dark and miserable all day, and the howling wind kept the storm clouds rolling like an angry sea. Out on the street, the wind-tossed poplars looked in serious danger of being uprooted, and fallen roof slates littered the pavement.

When the rain began, it was driven against the window panes with such force that I feared they might break. The doors rattled, the house creaked and the wind roared like a steam locomotive down the chimney.

I made up the fire with the intention of lighting it later, but it got really cold and Bogart was pacing uneasily, so I lit it, hoping the hypnotic effect of the flames would have a calming effect on him. In truth, I lit it for myself for the same reasons.

'Good day for a haunting, big fella, hey?' I teased him, stroking his back and neck. The comment, however glib, made me feel edgy. The fact was, I had felt a creeping

unease since the night before. An anxious, sickly feeling. A feeling of something unpleasant impending. I tried to shake it off, but it stayed with me, clinging like a shitty blanket.
I hoped that the fire would cheer us both up.

I was troubled by the video I'd seen and the uncanny coincidence between what Beth had said and the haunting by the boy, Zachary. Exactly how far into the pregnancy had Beth terminated? Why did she have an abortion if she'd planned all along to be a mother? Did the aborted foetus have a soul? Why did he appear as a child of various ages and why was he haunting me and not his mother? Was I predisposed to such things? I couldn't remember any other paranormal incidents in my life; could it be my state of mind that had made me susceptible to being haunted?

My head spun with enormity of it; so many unanswered questions. But I needed answers. The relief I'd felt after seeing Beth and bringing my worst fears to a head had been temporary and short-lived.

Chapter Forty Nine

Clara

Clara closed the door on number thirty-eight Burlington Road for the very last time. Unshed tears blurred her vision and her hands shook as she struggled with the key in the lock.

'Here Mum, let me.' Her son smiled tenderly at her, as though he had realised for the first time how old his mother had become. They walked together down the path to the front of the house, and Clara stopped and fished out a handkerchief from her bag and blew her nose.

'I'll give you a minute, Mum,' Michael said patiently.

Clara knew that Michael felt sad to be pulling her away from the home she had known and loved for many years, but the time had come for her to leave. The house was too big for her, besides; she was desperately lonely and her aggressive arthritis meant she would soon need a full time carer.

The house was to be sold, and she would live with him and his family in Norfolk. She was to have her own rooms in an annexe, so she could have as much company as she wanted while still retaining some of her independence. It was the perfect solution.

Clara stood looking up at the house, at the only home she had ever really known. She noticed the peeling paint and the grimy windows. The weeds and the overgrown lawn, the unkempt hedgerow blown about in the wind.

'Someone will take better care of you than I can,' she sniffed, wiping away the tears with her glove.

'Come on, Grandma.' Two small voices called out in unison from the back of the car. 'Let's go home.'

'Goodbye, Ted, my love,' Clara sighed and then turned towards the car. 'I'm coming,' she said. 'Hold on now, Grandma's coming.'

Inside the house, the curtains moved slightly, caught in a draught from the ill-fitting windows. The dust settled and the shadows, tempted from their corners, stretched out as though waking up cramped after a long, long sleep. All was still and silent within but for the wind that howled down the chimney and rattled the old windows, loose in their casements. Soon, even that died down, as if it had blown itself out and was conserving energy for the storm yet to come.

Only the persistent drip of a kitchen tap whose washer no-one had been there to fix could be heard now from the old woman's house. That and a whisper from somewhere within, ever so hushed, ever so gentle.

'Goodbye, Clara,' it said.

Chapter Fifty

The Meldrews

Margaret was glad to be home. She ran a hot bath and settled into the tub, covering herself with bubbles until only her eyes and the top of her head were visible. Let Jeremy see to the dogs for a change, she thought. He'd wanted the bloody things after all.

She knew she'd been distant with him lately and she felt bad about it. He'd been worried about her in the car on the way home and fearful about getting them home safely. In truth, she'd quite enjoyed the journey through the narrow, winding country lanes with the rain making the way hazardous and slippery and the wind buffeting against them.

She half wished the caravan had been smashed to smithereens and the dogs had died of fright. No! No, that was cruel! Cruel and unnecessary. But she had relished the element of danger. It was the most excitement she'd had for years. She had come close to feeling what was the word? Horny... Yes she had. Almost!

She remembered Jeremy's old car and their illicit lovemaking in public places. Deserted car parks, area's of wasteland where people walked their dogs, local beauty spots.

The greater the risk of getting caught, the more it turned her on. Jeremy had never been too comfortable with it, and the thought of that had thrilled her even more.

She knew she wasn't in love with Jeremy. They were chalk and cheese and always had been. Once, when they were younger, he'd tried impressing her by smoking pot.
She still laughed at the thought of him purple in the face, eyes protruding as he coughed and spluttered. Afterwards he'd been sick, and she'd felt guilty for being disappointed in him. Poor Jeremy! He'd never been what she had needed in a man. His idea of excitement was taking a different route home from the supermarket.

She thought of her neighbour, Alan, and her pulse quickened; inasmuch as she had appreciated watching a bare-chested Joaquin putting up a new fence in his garden, and even the cute, boyish charms of Jared had not been wasted on her, she couldn't help but melt whenever she thought of Alan. He reminded her of Gregory Peck, tall, handsome and distinguished, gentle yet manly, kind but strong and passionate. Her heart turned somersaults at the mere thought of him.

Her hand reached down and she stroked her inner thigh, sighing as she thought of Alan's strong hands caressing her. She had always been a physical woman, and Jeremy had hardly come close to satisfying her, even in their younger days. She drew her tongue across her lips as she imagined Alan making passionate love to her. Sturdy, silent Alan, with his kind grey eyes and dark wavy hair. Alan, who knew how to fill a suit. Alan, with his immaculately polished shoes and the collar of his overcoat turned up against the biting wind.

'Oh, Alan,' she murmured, sinking lower into the hot water.

She had always admired him from afar, but recently her feelings for him were something akin to love. She felt, all of a sudden, an overwhelming urgency to tell him, to bring things to a head. Even if that meant losing Jeremy.

She jumped out of the bath and looked at herself in the full length mirror. I still have it, she thought. Her body was firm and supple and her hair was good and thick. She had all her own teeth and barely a wrinkle to show for all the years she'd spent washing Jeremy's underpants. She took off her shower cap and her hair cascaded down her back in waves. Although it was more salt and pepper now, she could remember a time when it resembled the spun gold of a fairytale princess.

She quickly dried herself and found out the sexy red dress she'd bought when she was planning to take up salsa. Jeremy never knew of course and she'd ended up not going, but she'd kept the dress as a reminder of her intention to start living again. She ran her fingers through her hair, rouged her cheeks and painted her lips with passionate cherry. On the way out she passed Jeremy on the stairs.

'Where are *you* going?' he cried. 'The dogs are wanting their supper.'

Margaret stopped suddenly and backtracked. She stood in front of Jeremy, their faces so close that he could smell the sweetness of her skin, the scented afterglow of her bath. He could see her cherry lips, her rouged cheeks. She glowered at him. It looked for a second as if she might hit him.

'Fuck the dogs!' she said, her voice like gravel. 'I'm going to make mad, passionate love to Alan.'

*****

'Margaret,' Alan cried out in astonishment when he opened the door to her. 'What a pleasant surprise. Is there anything wrong?'

Alan didn't look at all well, but Margaret was on a mission. She brushed passed him and swept into the hallway. He had never seen her like this before, he couldn't help but thinking what a handsome woman she was.

'Alan' she said, in a hushed whisper. 'I have something to tell you, something I need to get off my chest. I…I…' She found herself lost for words.

'What is it Margaret?' Alan said, the concern evident in his voice. 'Is it Jeremy? Is he ill?'

'Do you think I might have a drink Alan? A stiff sherry perhaps?'

Alan watched bemused as Margaret threw back her sherry. He didn't even know she liked a drink. Margaret felt reckless, excited. She had dropped her coat on the floor and thrown herself against his chest. This was her Casablanca moment and he was her Rick.

'Alan I…' She stood, offering him the glass and then held on to it tightly, like a precious something he was trying to take away. 'Alan, I love you. I have always loved you. Your wide shoulders, your twinkling eyes, the way you smile. Oh, Alan, make love to me!'

Alan grabbed her wrists and tried to unpeel her, his discomfort at her proximity far outweighing his shock at her confession.

'Margaret, *please*!' he said, not unkindly. 'Please sit down.' They sat next to one another on the sofa and turned so they were facing. His knee brushed hers and she felt herself go weak at the contact. He took her hands in his and looked deep into her eyes.

'Margaret.' He smiled, 'we have known each other for a long time and you know I am very fond of you.' He cleared his throat. 'You and Jeremy both. But Margaret, you know this could never be.'

'But…' Margaret interrupted, tears stinging her eyes.

'Margaret, dear, kind, lovely Margaret. You are still a very handsome woman but…well, if you are unhappy in your marriage, then that's for you to sort out with Jeremy or maybe it's time to move on, but Marg…'

'*Alan!*' she pleaded. It came out as a whine.

Alan took both of her hands in his as though they were coming together in prayer. Then he gently kissed her fingertips.

'Margaret, I can't love you...' he said softly. 'I'm gay.'

Margaret gasped and pulled her hands away as if she'd been bitten.

'I know it's hard and I know it's painful.'

She stared at him in horror. Alan, the epitome of manhood. Alan so tall and strong!

'I too love someone I'll never be able to have.'

She held her hand to her mouth, trying to suppress a sob. Tears trickled freely down her face. She looked at Alan for a moment, her eyes wide. He dropped his head.

'I'm so sorry Margaret,' he whispered. 'So very sorry.' He covered his own eyes in a bid to stop the tears from rolling down his face. His voice cracked. 'I've been disappointing people my whole life, I know.'

Margaret jumped up from the couch and fled. Jeremy stood anxiously in the doorway waiting for her to come home.

'Oh Jeremy,' she sobbed and fell into his open arms.

'Come on, Maggie May,' he said, kissing her hair. 'The kettle's on. I'll make us a nice mug of Ovaltine.'

Chapter Fifty One

Beth sat opposite me on the sofa. Her towel-dried hair hung in loose curls around her face. With both hands tightly wrapped around a steaming mug of coffee, she stared distractedly into the fire. Before calling my ex-wife, I had called my mother and as soon as I'd asked after her and my father, I quickly cut in before her interrogation could begin.

'Sylvia…' I began, deciding that where my mother was concerned the direct approach was best. 'Had I ever claimed to have seen a ghost when I was a child?' I was surprised when she laughed.

'Jared,' she cried. 'Jared! You were always seeing ghosts. You had an incredible imagination. Not only did you see them, you had conversations with them. One in particular you had, an imaginary friend, you played with him all the time…Oh dear, now what was his name, Jebadiah? No, Zachariah… No, no. Zachary! That's right; your imaginary friend was called Zachary.'

'Why the sudden need to talk, Jared?' said Beth. 'And why couldn't you come to me? I've so much do before I go.'

I didn't feel the need in discussing my fear of leaving the house with the person I felt was responsible in some way for it; instead, I directed the questions straight back at her.

'Why couldn't you tell me you were pregnant Beth, and why abort behind my back?   Was it someone else's baby?'

'Christ, Jared,' she snapped, taking a cigarette from a packet in her coat pocket. 'Oh, sorry, do you mind if I smoke?' I shook my head and she took a long, thin, gold lighter from her bag.

I watched her trying to light up with trembling fingers, and I took the lighter from her and struck the wheel. An instant flare illuminated Beth's tired, gaunt face as she leant forward with her cigarette.

Our fingers met briefly as I handed back the lighter, but it was a temporary blip. A thing of little consequence. Beth dragged on the cigarette, breathing in long and hard before releasing. The smoke curled in-between us, a blue gossamer veil beneath which lovers might have shared a first kiss.

'Sorry,' I said. 'But it needed asking.'

'Did it?' she replied irritably.

'But why, Beth?' I knew it was a question that would have reduced her to tears only last week, but now her eyes were dry as though she had no more tears left to cry.

'Our marriage, it was going nowhere, Jared. I felt stifled by it, trapped! I tried talking to you many times, but you never bloody listened.'

She looked at me as if expecting me to protest; when I remained silent, she carried on.

'In a few years time we will be forty. We'd have still been living in this house, you'd still be a jingle writer and I'd still be PA to someone far less able and competent than myself. I have ambition, but trying to have the drive for both of us, it wore me out, it held me back, Jared, and I resented you for it.' She put the cigarette down and held my two hands in hers.

'Look at you! Looking at me with those puppy dog eyes, you big dope.' She smiled. 'I love you, Jared, I always will. But I need adventure. I need to live life to the full. Surely you can understand that?'

I nodded.

'I couldn't be tied down with another baby. I already had you to look after.'

I put my head in her lap like I used to and she ran her fingers through my hair.

'Why didn't you tell me?' I said.

'Because you would have tried to stop me, Jared; and you would have succeeded. I would have stayed and I would have hated you for it.'

I knew she was right. Deep within my heart I knew and I fully understood why she had to go. It hurt like hell. But at last I understood.

Beth and I stayed like that for a long time, after which we hugged and then shared a drink for old times' sake.

'Oh…' I said, suddenly remembering. 'I found this upstairs.' I handed her the tape and she gave a cry of surprise.

'Dear God…' she said. 'I thought it was lost forever. Can I?'

She watched her bridal shower tape through blurred, teary eyes and amid much laughter, and I watched her with a heavy heart, because I remembered why I loved her and I knew how much I'd miss her. Bogart came and joined us, and the three of us watched television together as if nothing had changed. But it had changed, irrevocably and we both knew there was no going back.

As she was leaving the house for the very last time, I asked her about the cushion, the 'bump,' and why she'd said what she had said.

'It was a long time ago…' she said with a smile. 'And I was very drunk, but I think somewhere deep down, I did want to have children with you someday.'

I walked her to the front door, and opening it, I said, 'A child. Just one!'

'Yes.' She smiled as she was closing the car door. 'A boy. Zachary, after your imaginary childhood friend.'

Chapter Fifty Two

Beth

Beth arrived at the airport with time to spare.

She was going to New Zealand until she decided what she really wanted from her life. Strangely enough, rather than feeling good about not only getting away, but with Jared's best wishes too, she felt nervous. No! Terrified would be more appropriate.

Was she doing the right thing? She thought of them all cuddled up watching television. She missed Jared, Bogart and their little home terribly. Was it too late to go back? No, she couldn't do that to Jared. She loved him too much! She had no doubt that within a week she would be feeling stifled again, as though her life were already over. No, she had to move on. It was the only way.

Her hand trembled a little as she rifled through her bag, checking on her tickets for the millionth time. There were a good few people around. Families with excited children off on late season package holidays, couples on romantic breaks to far flung destinations and other lone travellers, probably taking business trips. In an adjacent queue, a man in a suit caught her eye and winked at her. She ignored him and turned back towards the flight desks.

How many of those around her were leaving for a new life? Where were they going? How many more would be returning home with their tails between their legs, penniless, having failed in their new ventures? We're not all Joaquins, she thought smiling, born nomads.

After checking in, she wandered around the airport's shops for a little while. She felt desperately lonely. Should she phone Jared and let him know where she was going? No, she should let him go. He'd done her the courtesy of letting her move on with her life and she needed to do the same for him. After all, divorce proceedings had already started. She couldn't leave him hanging on while she decided whether a life of new adventures was the one for her or not, and besides, didn't he have a new woman already? Now what was that bitch's name…Rebecca? No, Rachel. That was it. *'Had to dash, last night was wonderful… love Rachel x'*

She subconsciously pulled a pair of sunglasses from a rack in front of her. She felt a stab of jealousy when she remembered the note, and Jared had offered no explanation. But then, he didn't owe her one did he? She'd deserted him, aborted his child and then asked for a divorce.

She felt tears spill down her cheeks and she wiped them away impatiently. Pull yourself together woman, she reprimanded, replacing the designer sunglasses back on the rack. She decided she needed a drink, badly! Picking up her hand luggage, she walked towards the gate through to departures and her new life.

Chapter Fifty Three

Joaquin

Joaquin thought how much the woman he had just seen go through the departure lounge security gate looked like his friend Beth. Bit skinnier perhaps, hair a bit longer, but a striking resemblance nonetheless.

The flight had been delayed by four hours, meaning he would not reach Burlington until late. It had been hot and crowded, and he was extremely tired and anxious. I'm getting too old for this, he thought. He felt surprised by the admission, as though the idea had just crept into his mind, or been suggested to him by someone else.

Although he loved seeing the world, he was becoming increasingly intolerant of roughing it and bumming rides here, there and everywhere. He realised that for the first time ever he missed his comfortable little house. Ironically, for the first time, he would not be able to return there.

He suddenly felt alone, homeless and alienated, and he was shocked by these new feelings and the need in him to be grounded. It went against the very grain of him. Could he really be tired of travelling and ready to settle? It seemed so implausible.

He looked out of the main terminal window. In the distance he could see a chain of lights and for a second or two he could not understand why they seemed to be moving about with such force and then, as if in answer to his question, a sudden spray of rain hit the glass. It seemed as though the storm clouds were following him.

He thought again of his friend and wondered at the feelings of dread and anxiety he felt, whenever he did so. Was Alan in any danger? It seemed unlikely, but one thing was for certain; something at Burlington was terribly wrong.

Chapter Fifty Four

The storm raged all the next day. By 5pm, the night had set in and it hadn't abated any.

In fact, it had gotten worse.

I had spent the day in front of the television, watching re-runs of 'Only Fools and Horses,' anything to take away this anxious, uneasy feeling. After seeing Beth again, I realised it was time to move on. I knew my life needed direction, because I was well and truly lost and Beth wouldn't be there to lean on anymore. I felt alone and afraid, but this feeling of unease, of dread was something else altogether.

Bogart had attempted to go out twice, but the weather had driven him back indoors. He sat around morose, watching the rain-soaked garden from the French doors. I picked him up and hugged him, relishing his warmth. A sudden shower of hailstone hit the window with such force that he tried to jump out of my arms.

'What's happening out there, wildcat?' I said in hushed tones, trying to soothe him. 'Four seasons in one day, hey? Guess that's what happens when you screw up the planet, Humph, eh?'

The cat was in no mood for humouring. He jumped from my arms and plodded over to the fire, standing and looking at the flames for a while, before making a nest in the rug and settling down in it. I went around checking the doors were locked, a habit I'd gotten into with the coming of the early dark nights.

I was about to make a hot drink when the cellar door shot open. I was still trying to convince myself that Zachary was a product of my imagination or a bi-product of too much gin and Prozac, so I quickly shut it again, cursing the draughty old cellar and the knackered lock. Nevertheless, I shuddered as I turned the key, my apprehension deepening by the minute.

I reminded myself that Joaquin would be back soon and that my life was about to get on track again. I was still youngish. I was solvent. I had so much more to look forward to.

Feeling a little cheered, I decided to open a bottle of South African red. Joaquin's favourite, I reminded myself grabbing the bottle and a glass and making my way into the lounge.

Just before midnight I awoke. Cold and aching, my mouth was dry and my head groggy. The fire had long since died down, and Bogart as usual had left me and gone to bed. I didn't feel as though I'd been asleep. I was exhausted but I knew the chances of going back to sleep were virtually nil. Half awake but weary, I made my way to the bathroom where I swallowed four Diazepam with a glass of water. By the time my head hit the pillow, I was dead to the world. I didn't hear the taxi pull up, taking Rachel back home. Nor did I see every light turned on in Chez Joaquin, or hear the commotion as Simeon's mistress was dragged, naked and screaming, into the street by the incensed wife. I was lost in a bottomless, far-away chemical oblivion, too deep to be roused by the disturbances only a door away, too deep even for the dreams that would otherwise haunt my sleeping hours.

I was lost to the world, and my oblivion was complete and very, very welcome.

Chapter Fifty Five

Rachel

Simeon had already decided that his marriage was over. If only his wife would come back, he would tell her so. As it was, he didn't even know where she was, and she'd taken his son away.

He hadn't meant to hit her; he'd just gone too far. Not that it was unmerited. Since they'd moved to Burlington Road, she had been an A grade bitch. Actually she had always been. It used to turn him on, but since he'd been foolish with their nest egg, she'd been a nasty, condescending A grade bitch. Pulling him down, belittling him every chance she got. Hell, he hadn't done it on purpose, gambled it away, pissed it up the walls. True, it had been a bad business decision, but done with the best of intentions - to keep his madam of a wife in the style she was accustomed to.

He relaxed on the bed. Fuck you, Rachel, he thought, pinching the top of his nose between his forefinger and thumb. You've given me a headache for the last time.

'Sarah… Ms. Jones. I'm getting cold,' he called out. 'Where are you?'

'Patience, my love.' A tall, leggy blonde entered the bedroom wearing nothing but his shirt and a smile. In her hand she carried a silver tray with a bottle of Dom Perignon and two glasses.

'Steady with that, my girl' he cautioned. 'Money doesn't grow on trees you know.'

'This one's on me,' she purred, leaning forward so that her ample breasts slipped free of the shirt. 'And so is this.'

She placed the tray on the bed, and he saw the two lines of white powder she'd laid out.

'Now you are *really* spoiling me,' he said with a grin, cupping her breast with his hand so that she moaned aloud. He took out a crisp note from his wallet and rolled it into a straw, taking the powder up his nose, before laying back and sighing with pleasure.

'My turn,' his mistress cried petulantly, grabbing for the note.

Suddenly, the door was thrown open with such force that the couple jumped, white powder and champagne spilling all over. Rachel stood over Sarah, her arms crossed.

'You cow!' Sarah screamed, hurling herself at a shocked Rachel, who grabbed her by the hair and dragged her off the bed.

'So you're the junkie slut who's screwing my husband?' Rachel yelled. Getting Sarah in a head lock, she dragged her across the floor and out into the landing. Sarah was a poor match for Rachel, and in her current half-cut state, even less so. Rachel hauled the screaming woman down the stairs, wrinkling up her nose in disgust as Simeon's shirt rode up, revealing his mistress's naked loins.

At the bottom of the stairs, Sarah found her feet and turned to face Rachel, hissing and spitting bile. Rachel slapped her hard across the face, and Sarah stood shocked for a moment, before reaching for Rachel's eyes with her fingernails.

'RACHEL!' She could hear Simeon bundling about upstairs.

'Simeon!' Sarah wailed as Rachel grabbed her by the hair, twisting Sarah around as she did so.

'GET OUT OF MY HOUSE, YOU BITCH!' Rachel screamed at Sarah, opening the front door and throwing her husband's mistress out into the storm-tossed street. Sarah hammered at the door Rachel slammed in her face.

'Give me my clothes, you old cow. GIVE ME MY CLOTHES!'

At the sudden noise behind her, Rachel looked over her shoulder to see Simeon teetering at the top of the stairs.

'RACHEL,' he bellowed, rocking unsteadily on his feet. He lost his balance and came crashing down towards her. Rachel jumped to one side, and he landed at her feet with such force, she felt sure he must be dead. For a moment she was dazed, and then she panicked. Climbing over her husband's slumped body, she raced upstairs and into their bedroom. She grabbed Sarah's clothes, walking them carefully downstairs and stepping over her husband's prone body.

Sarah had stopped banging and was wailing at the door.

'Simeon! Please Simeon!'

Rachel opened the door a fraction, just enough to push Sarah's clothes out onto the rain-soaked porch. Five minutes later, she heard the car pull away.

Chapter Fifty Six

I sensed rather than saw the figure at the end of my bed. Bogart pawed the air and then hissed, arching his back and digging his claws deep into the duvet, and in turn, into my leg. I cried out, the pain rousing me from my drug-induced stupor, any remains of drowsiness instantly vanished.

A sudden gust of wind hit with such violence that the whole building shook. Outside, the lights went out and I was glad to be in my sturdy, little house rather than some new-build, high rise with paper walls. We'd withstood the Luftwaffe; let the wind do its worst. I was suddenly aware of an icy chill within the room, so cold that I shivered inside my duvet. I could see my hot breath misting in the frozen air, but the air wasn't still. I could just make out movement amid the shadows, and I had a strong feeling I was being watched. All at once, a feeling of great urgency overpowered me, overcoming any fear I had for the unearthly figure that I knew lurked in the darkness. Then I saw him. I saw him clearly. It was Zachary, and the expression on his face chilled me to the bone.

Suddenly, the cellar door flew open with such force that I jumped out of my skin. Bogart fled, bolting through the bedroom door and tearing downstairs as if his tail were on fire. I grabbed my jeans from the bottom of the bed and followed suit, my heart pounding against my ribcage. When

I reached the bottom, the wind subsided abruptly, and I heard a blood-curdling scream, so piercing, it rent the night air like a dagger. I panicked, feeling useless and vulnerable. My skin prickled with fear and my breathing was laboured.

Zachary stood at the foot of the stairs, his expression fearful and pleading.

'Go, Jared, go,' he begged me. I heard him clearly, but I couldn't move.

'Jared…Go, please,' he moaned in despair.

Then, the chilling scream came again and I knew without a shadow of doubt that it was Rachel and that she was in grave danger.

'I think he wants to kill me!'

The memory of her standing in my kitchen, the fear clearly etched into her face, the tears streaming down her cheek, suddenly spurred me into action.

'Help me, Zachary' I cried out, and I was able to move. I raced toward the front door, unlocking it and pulling it open in one swift movement…and then it hit me, like an iron fist.

The street widened and leaned at an irregular angle. My head spun and I had to grab the doorframe to steady myself. All was silent at Chez Joaquin now. The storm had died down and the street was bathed in an eerie orange glow.

'Zachary, help me,' I cried out in frustration.

'A journey begins with the first step, Jared.' I heard the voice inside my head this time. It was Zachary's voice.

I stepped forward gingerly and waited for the ground to rush up and hit me. It didn't! I took another step and then another and before I knew it, I'd reached the bottom of the path. The street looked as it always had, regular and safe. I cried out with relief.

Then came a sudden loud crash from number thirty-seven and all at once, I was out of the gate and running the short distance between my house and Rachel's. The door was ajar and the darkness within seemed solid.

'Rachel,' I screamed. 'Rachel, where are you?'

I heard what sounded like a whimper coming from the kitchen. The sound was restricted, weak, as if coming from a compressed windpipe. A sudden fury overcame me and I ran up the hallway, screaming, and hurled myself at the kitchen door.

The room looked like a bombsite. The table and chairs were over-turned and broken. Glassware, dishes and utensils were spread across the floor. Cupboard doors had been pulled open, some yanked off their hinges, and the cupboards' contents, packets and jars were strewn across the worktops.

The storm hit again with violence and a flash of lightning bleached the scene. In one corner, stood Rachel and her husband. She was pinned against the wall, her legs collapsing from under her; he had his hands wrapped tightly around her throat, his thumbs applying pressure to her trachea. Her eyes protruded from her head and her tongue lolled. She was already blue from lack of oxygen, and the rattle that came from her throat told me I might already be too late.

He seemed oblivious to me, and I came up behind him and brought my elbow down hard and fast against his lower spine. He screamed out in anger and pain, letting go of Rachel, who slid to the floor. For a moment I thought she was dead. She lay there not moving. Then she gasped, and I cried out with relief.

'Jared?' she whispered and then winced with pain at the attempt.

'Ssshhh,' I told her. 'Try not to talk. You'll be fine now.'

I saw her eyes widen with fear and she struggled to move, her breaths coming laboured and sharp. I turned on reflex, moving my head slightly so I avoided the full force of the blow that was coming my way. I looked into the eyes of a madman. Drugged eyes. Eyes that were wild with hatred. His fist caught me on the bridge of the nose and blood erupted from it like lava from a volcano. The room spun for a moment as the pain shot across my forehead, and I shook my head as if trying to shake the dizziness out, blood spraying across Simeon's crisp, white robe.

I almost gagged as the blood poured down the back of my throat, and Simeon took his chance and came at me again. This time I ducked and he smashed his hand hard against the wall. With madness, hatred and God only knows what narcotics fuelling him, he spun around, but I seized the opportunity and caught him off balance, a swift right uppercut making contact with his jaw. I heard the bone crack, and his knees crumpled as I followed with a punch to the side of his head.

Rachel had managed to crawl away, and I had Simeon cornered. I could feel the adrenalin pumping. I felt alive again. I stepped back, and Simeon put his arms up to protect his head.

'Enough, enough,' he managed to slur. He spat out blood on the kitchen floor, and I realised he had bitten through his tongue when I punched him on the jaw. He lay dazed in the corner from the blows to his head and I went over to Rachel. Her breathing had eased, but there was a nasty mark on her throat. She would be sore for a few days, but she would recover. She smiled at me.

'Hello, Jared Colne,' she said. She closed her eyes, her ordeal obviously having exhausted her, and I tried to stand. My own head was swimming, but I needed to call an ambulance and the boys in blue.

The next thing I knew was a sharp crack, just behind my ear. It felt as though my skull had split. I felt a vicious pain shoot across the top of my head and I saw a blinding white light, but not for long. The darkness spread across my vision like black ink in water, gradually cutting out the light, and for the second time in just a few hours, oblivion opened up her velvet cloak and welcomed me into her arms.

Chapter Fifty Seven

Joaquin

Joaquin was almost on Burlington Road when the lights went out.

He felt breathless, his mouth dry, but his back was soaking with the exertion of trying to make it home from the station. He could sense that something was wrong. He could taste it. The atmosphere was charged, and when he turned into Burlington Road, it looked like a scene from a horror film. Every house seemed quiet and deserted, and in-between flashes of lightning, the darkness seemed absolute.

He looked across at Graham's, but oddly there was no car in the drive. The trembling trees seemed to reach out their branches as if to embrace him, but this didn't feel like a welcome home. He shivered. A sudden flash of lightning illuminated number forty, and he could have sworn he saw someone moving about within its darkened, empty rooms.

All he could hear above the howling wind was the distant sound of sirens, a creaking For Sale sign outside Clara's house, and his own heartbeat. He turned to look over the hill at the outlying town, a sudden lash of rain stinging his eyes. He saw smoke on the horizon, and an orange glow told him that something in town had received a direct lightning strike.

His legs felt like legs do in dreams, when it seems the dreamer is wading through treacle. Time seemed to be winding down, while his heart beat faster and faster. He finally reached Alan's door and knocked loudly, urgently crying out Alan's name when no-one answered.

Joaquin peered anxiously through Alan's kitchen window. All was silent inside the house. He toyed with the idea of breaking in, but everything seemed in order and there was no sign of any intruder or any struggle. Why would there be? Alan was probably out of town. It wasn't unusual. Alan travelled around almost as much as Joaquin himself.

He tried his phone, but it seemed the landlines were down and he couldn't hear his mobile ringing inside the house. Alan simply wasn't home. No-one seemed to be at home on Burlington. Still, it was late; he could always try again tomorrow. He walked around the front and knocked one last time.

'Alan,' he called out. 'It's me, Joaquin.' Only silence from inside; the house was empty.

Chapter Fifty Eight

Alan

You are getting your affairs together and making sure everything is in order before your departure. You've left your home and anything of value to your favourite charity and a few personal effects to Joaquin. You know you will never see him again.

You are becoming extremely forgetful, the day, the month, the year. You hope you remembered to cancel your papers.

For the last couple of days you have been feeling really tired, and you are fairly sure you're hallucinating. You woke up this morning and your bedroom was full of cats, and although your eyesight is failing, you keep stepping over imaginary trip wires that you see stretched across your stairs.

Any given day could be your last, so you have shaved and groomed in preparation. You hope to have time to finish your book, Leonard Cohen's Book of Longing, before you go. Not only was it a gift from Joaquin, you also find it soothing and beautifully written. They say you never forget the person who introduced you to Leonard Cohen. You know you will never forget Joaquin. You never did read his letter, what would be the point? You wonder where he is now, what he's doing and who he's doing it with.

You feel strangely calm and peaceful, if not a little dizzy. The room seems to be swaying as though you are slightly drunk. It's not wholly unpleasant. You think you might want to drink your last glass of wine and have a sudden urge to listen to Madam Butterfly. You think of Margaret and her touching admission of love for you and smile at the irony of it. Margaret's unrequited love for you, your unrequited love for Joaquin. Who would you pity the most?

You suddenly feel incredibly tired. The music has built to a crescendo although it sounds as if it's being played underwater. Suddenly it stops and the lights go out. You drop your wine glass and it falls silently onto the beige carpet, staining it a deep, blood red. The glass rolls a little before coming to rest against the leg of the coffee table.

You lay back and rest your eyes, just for a while. All is peaceful; you are cocooned in warmth like in the womb. Everything is fading now, even the sound of the storm, although you are certain you can hear someone hammering at your door and the voice of the one you love calling out your name. You open your eyes; still everything is dark and the silence is complete and safe. No distant cars, no howling wind, not even the sound of your own heartbeat. You can still hear Joaquin calling, and you know the sound of his voice will live on forever in your memory.

The darkness is not solid; you can just make out shadowy figures in the distance. The figures take on the form of your parents and grandparents, and theirs are the voices that call you now.

'Come home, Alan,' they cry in unison. 'Come home now.'

On the horizon you can just make out a pinprick of brilliant white light. It seems to be getting bigger, but then you realise it's a lamp or something like and it's moving, getting closer. A hand reaches out and grabs yours, and you look up into the smiling face of your father.

'I was never disappointed in you, son,' he says.

Chapter Fifty Nine

Lisa had managed to grip the nail file she'd shoved into the back pocket of her lounge pants when she'd gone to answer the door. It seemed like hours she'd been working at the rope. Her wrist was bloodied where she caught it with the sharpened end, and her fingers were numbed with the effort. Finally, the rope gave, and she groaned as she tried to stretch the stiffness from her tired, aching limbs.

She quickly untied her ankles, loosely re-wrapping the rope to make it look as though she were still bound, and placed her hands behind her back, gripping the file in her clenched fist.

Then she bowed her head, closed her eyes and waited.

Joaquin stepped out onto the street. His anxiety had eased a little; it seemed Alan was in no immediate danger, but he still felt tense and uneasy. Maybe he was just tired and wanted to be home.

He thought he might give Jared and Beth a tap. It was late, but they liked to burn the midnight oil. He could do with a drink and he could ask them about Alan. He was sure he would be fine; it felt better somehow, just being back on

Burlington. He should visit Clara too. He couldn't believe she was selling up.

He looked fondly at his old homestead. Strange, he thought. It looked in the shadows as if the front door was open. He was just about to walk up Jared path's when something wrapped itself around his legs, startling him. He looked down in alarm and saw a pair of yellow eyes looking up at him.

'Hey, Duke!' he cried. He always called the cat Duke after Bogart's character in The Petrified Forest. He was secretly relieved to see him and wondered at his own nervousness. When he knelt down, the cat nuzzled up to him. 'Whatya doing out in this, big fella?' he asked, rubbing Bogart's ears vigorously. 'C'mon lets get you in.'

He stood with the intention of knocking on the door of forty-one, but Bogart rushed ahead of him and went straight in. Peering through the gloom, he noticed that the door was open.

'Jared,' he called out from the doorstep. 'JARED! BETH!' He looked into the shadowy hallway and froze when he saw a pale-faced boy, watching him from the foot of the stairs.

'Lisa. Lisa wake up. I've brought you some food.'

Graham set the tray down at her feet, and Lisa knew he'd see the ropes hanging loosely from her ankles. In a flash, she was up. Catching a crouching Graham off balance, she leapt forward and brought her forehead down with force on the bridge of his nose. She almost screamed with the pain, but Graham was down. His nose, clearly broken, had literally burst, and his face was a bloody mask. His glasses had cracked and lay on the floor beside him. She kicked them away, knowing he was nearly blind without them.

'You bitch,' he groaned, rolling about the floor. 'Bitch! You...'

Lisa made for the door. She knew he locked it after he left and was hoping he'd left the key in. He had! Turning it in the lock until it clicked, she pocketed it and ran upstairs.

'LISA!' she heard him bellow as he threw himself against the door.

'Joaquin? JOAQUIN!' Margaret squealed, and he turned to find a torch shining directly into his face. He blinked and shielded his eyes from the glare.

'It is you. It is him, Jeremy! Oh Joaquin, I thought it was. Come in, love. Come in out of the rain.'

'Hi, Margaret. Yes, I'm back. Oh, hi, Jeremy. Erm... where is everybody? Jared's door is wide open. I was just about to check if they're ok.'

'Be careful, Joaquin,' Margaret said, pulling her robe tightly around her chest. 'It's been terrible here tonight, what with the screams and the blackouts and...'

'Screams? From Jared's?' He moved toward the door. 'JARED?' he called. 'BETH?' He was about to go in when Margaret's strangulated scream stopped him.

'Margaret? What the hell is going on?' he asked, turning. Margaret had swooned and was being supported by Jeremy. Her face was ashen and she could barely speak, and her hand trembled as she pointed over to number forty. In the living room window, Joaquin saw a face, pale and ghostly, its expression one of cold fear. He looked back at Margaret, who had passed out in her husband's arms.

When he glanced back to the house, the face had gone.

Lisa fumbled for the latch on the back door and found it locked.

'Damn it!' she cursed, almost jumping out of her skin when Graham hurled himself at the cellar door with an enormous thud. Desperate, she hunted for the key but couldn't find it anywhere. She ran to the front door. Locked. She almost wept with frustration and fear. It was then she remembered where her Granny used to keep her key, swearing no-one could find it but herself. Fingering around the door frame, Lisa gave a sob of relief when she felt the cold metal between her fingertips.

Jared

When I came to, I found myself tied back to back with Rachel, whose feet were fixed to a big iron ring in the floor, which opened a latch to the cellar. I could see Simeon standing over us. His Jack Nicolson Joker-grin hung at an odd angle from his face, and I realised with some satisfaction that his jaw was broken. His ear was ripped and bleeding, which I'm sure had nothing to do with me, and there seemed to be a dent in the side of his head. His white robe was covered in blood and his eyes stared manically from one of us to the other.

'You ruined my life, you ungrateful cow,' he slurred at Rachel, spitting blood everywhere from his mangled tongue. His words were hard to make out and he swayed dangerously, holding on to one of the barstools of the central island for support.

'Everything I did, I did for you and the boy,' he said, his eyes filming over, filled with tears.

'Simeon please,' Rachel begged. 'I still love you; we love you, me and Tris. We can get past this.'

'And who's this bastard?' He spat, kicking me in the ribs as he did so. The kick had little momentum.

'He's our neighbour,' she rasped through crushed vocal chords. 'He heard me screaming and came to help, that's all.'

Her eyes widened with fear as he pulled a lighter from his shirt pocket and began wafting it in her face. I thought for one moment that he would set her clothes alight, but he moved to the far side of the room, to the French windows.

'I never did like your taste in furnishings, Rach,' he smirked

'Help!' I yelled as the flames quickly took hold.

'Please, baby, please' sobbed Rachel. 'For Tris' sake.'

Simeon stayed, transfixed by the flames, making no attempts to move, even when a large piece of flaming swag broke away and landed close to his feet. Still, I wondered how he managed to stand upright, so perilously was he swaying.

He went to the under-stairs cupboard and pulled out a baseball bat. He came over to me and started swinging the bat. Insanity and hatred shone from his eyes and he laughed swinging closer to my head every time. This is it, I thought. I'm going to die! Rachel behind me had dropped her head, a low moaning coming from her throat.

'No, no. Please no, please no...'

I do not know if Joaquin saw the flames first or heard me yelling. All I know is that he suddenly appeared in the doorway as if by magic. Rachel saw him first and gasped. Simeon must have heard him coming because he hid behind the door, brandishing his bat and lying in wait. Rachel must have given some warning, because Joaquin stopped just short of the door. By this time he had been joined by Jeremy and Margaret, who fainted again when she saw Simeon fly at Joaquin, screaming and waving the bat above his head.

Joaquin never so much as blinked as the bat came down. He grabbed it and tore it from Simeon's grasp, bringing his foot up at the same time and kicking Simeon clean in the face with a shot Bruce Lee would have been proud of. Simeon went down like a pack of cards and Joaquin ran over to the curtains, tearing them down and stamping out the flames underfoot. Jeremy followed him in and untied Rachel and me, Rachel collapsing in his arms like a ragdoll. I tried to stand and go over to Joaquin. But as soon as I got to my knees the room began to sway. I could hear sirens right outside and people talking and suddenly the lights came back on. I stood using Jeremy's shoulder for support and was on my feet for all of three seconds when the floor rushed up and smacked me in the face.

The last thing I saw before I blacked out was Zachary, stood in the doorway smiling at me.

In the murky cellar of number forty, Graham whimpered, like a puppy on its first night away from its mother. He heard the sirens and scuttled away into the darkest corner, tears streaking his blood-stained face.

Even when he'd reached the wall, he dug his heels in and clawed with his fingers at the cold damp floor, pressing his back hard against the brickwork, willing it to swallow him up.

And as he curled into a foetal ball and hummed his favourite tune, the shadows gathered, reaching in for him and taking him into their embrace as if welcoming one of their own.

Five years later

The sun sets over the bay and I watch it from the balcony of my apartment. It is a balmy, late summer's evening and the sky is streaked with crimson and gold.

From where I sit, I can just make out the ships, docked like tiny dots on the horizon. Sometimes, when the passenger ships come close to the shore at sunset to rest anchor for the night, I can just make out the cabin windows like tiny squares of gold, and the sea around them sparkles with a thousand gems.

I put my computer down for a while and stand to stretch. I've been working on an important ad campaign for a very famous radio station. My deadline is looming large, but I've been working hard all day, so I'm chilling with a beer before my girlfriend comes round for dinner.

That's the beauty of working freelance and from home; you can be anywhere in the world and submit your work electronically. It suits me fine.

I spot Matteus cleaning the pool and whistle to him. He extends me the middle finger and we both laugh. Matty is the brother of my girlfriend, Cecile, and we rub along pretty well. I've been with my girl for almost a year now. I really like her, but after being stung once, I'm taking things steady this time.

I've just been reading a mail from Joaquin. He's sent me a picture of him, Rachel and the kids. I can't believe he's married and settled with kids! It would take a woman like Rachel to ground a man like Joaquin. But I still find it hard to believe sometimes. I've had strict instructions to visit them in Burlington Road soon and I'm thinking of taking Cecile. I think they'll all get along just fine, and it's about time she got to know my friends.

I suppose you're wondering how this all came about? Me, about on my travels, and Joaquin married and settled back in Burlington? And about the rest of my neighbours after that night five years ago?

You see, I never went out again after Beth left. At least, the *me* she left didn't! That Jared still lives at forty-one, still hides away in the shadows; waiting for the wife he cannot live without to return, and I look back at him now with varying degrees of pity and contempt.

That night five years ago, a new Jared was born, forged almost literally from the ashes of the old one.

I awoke from my fainting spell to find myself in my bed, at number forty-one. Bogart was laid at my feet and Joaquin was slumped in the armchair by the fireplace. Rachel had been taken to hospital with a bruised larynx, where she was being treated for shock and minor respiratory difficulties.

Simeon had been arrested, pending trial for two counts of attempted murder, grievous bodily harm and being in possession of class A narcotics. I later learned that the judge had found him arrogant and unrepentant. He was given ten years, with no hopes of an early parole.

It was a couple of days after the event that we learned of Alan's death. No-one knew he was ill. The shock of it reverberated around Burlington Road, and the pain of his loss was heartfelt and affected us all in some way. Even Bogart mooched on his patio for a few days, until he decided that he'd have to make do with me and Joaquin.

Joaquin, whom I had persuaded to stay, was probably affected most of all by Alan's death. He told me about Alan's declaration of love, and how he'd run away and then felt guilty, and that's the reason he came back. I told him I was sure that Alan knew he'd come back and that he would have forgiven him for leaving in that way.

I also told him that in coming back, he had saved our lives and how proud that would make Alan feel. He still grieved terribly, and I thought he might disappear to some holy retreat or other and we wouldn't see him again, but he didn't. He stayed and we helped each other through the pain of our losses, coming through at the other end stronger and closer than any brothers.

It seemed I was cured of my agoraphobia, which my doctor assures me was not really agoraphobia, simply depression. I weaned myself off the Prozac and, strangely enough, with Joaquin's help I began to drink less. It was he who taught me the difference between drinking for pleasure and drinking through need. So now I take enormous pleasure in having the occasional drink, knowing that I don't need it and that I can take it or leave it.

After hearing of Alan's death, Joaquin would disappear for hours on end. I always knew where he went, because to my great shame I followed him once. He would sit by Alan's grave and read to him from Leonard Cohen's Book of Longing. A book Alan never got time to finish.

As time passed, he visited there less and less. Probably because he saw more and more of Rachel, which was a good thing. At first, Rachel would go with him; they went for shorter and shorter periods, until finally they stopped going altogether. It was a healthy period of mourning and I'm sure Alan wouldn't have minded when it came to an end. I know he loved Joaquin deeply and that he would want to see him happy.

In time Joaquin moved in with Rachel at number thirty-seven.

'Seems I've come the full circle' he would say laughing.

Apparently, Rachel had fallen head over heels in love with him the moment she set eyes on him, which, even had he not emerged as our all-conquering-hero, did not come as a surprise to me.

I was happy when they moved in together, not just because I felt they were good and right for one another, but because my plans to travel the world were coming to fruition at that time. I would rent out forty-one and that, along with the wages I received from the radio station, would comfortably support me on my travels.

Around three years ago and more or less exactly two years to the day since they'd met, Joaquin and Rachel married. She was already pregnant, and Joaquin became a good father to Tris. I was best man for the couple, and I think that my happiness that day easily matched that of the bride and groom.

Beth was there, too, a little reluctantly it seemed, as she thought turning up with a new man in tow would upset me. It's nice to know she still cares about my feelings, but I know we all have to move on. As Joaquin would say, 'It's not enough living to learn; we must also learn to live.' Which is exactly what Beth taught me when she walked away from our marriage six years ago.

No regrets and no hard feelings. She moved to New York to work in a major publishing house. There she met Jim, her husband to be and she is very happy. I often think of her and our time together, and I also thank her for having the wisdom and courage to move on when the time was right. I'm still not sure I would have had the guts to do so myself at that time.

I also think of the child we made together, especially when I see Joaquin with his children. It makes me a little sad, but I'm still young enough to have more children one day.

Beth and I talk and mail each other regularly, and both Jim and Cecile are fine with it.
I think we'll always be close, not only for a love shared but for the valuable things we learned through being together and in separating.

Also at the wedding were Jeremy and Margaret, who seemed like newlyweds again themselves. Jeremy had known all along about Margaret's infatuation with Alan. He also knew that Alan was gay, but Margaret's actions that night had given him the shake-up he needed. After a couple of sherries at the reception and after hearing how sad and shocked she had been at finding out about our divorce, Margaret proceeded to tell me at great length about the secrets of 'spicing up' a tired marriage. I was mortified, and it was only when Jeremy jangled the keys of their new car, one 'Ford Zephyr,' that I was released from my hell.

Clara was invited to the ceremony too, but was not able to attend. I'm told by a reliable source (Margaret) that she's happy and well in her home by the sea and that she is adored by her two grand-children.

As for Graham, police broke into number forty later that morning to find him gone. The basement was full of rubble sacks and different kinds of poison, along with piles of tinned dog and cat food. He had been luring animals, foxes mainly, the odd stray dog, into his garden with the poisoned food and then dumping their bodies into an old quarry in the woods.

He was found a week later, wandering half-starved and half-naked on the hard-shoulder of the M1. He was taken to a secure psychiatric hospital, where I believe after four years of intensive therapy, he is now much improved. He still claims to have no recollection of that night whatsoever, not the kidnap, the fire or the restaurant. We can only hope he's more peaceful now and will at some point be able to assume a normal life.

Lisa, just for the record, recovered well from her ordeal and went on to marry Slimy Simon, the redundant office clerk, who'd found a much better job elsewhere. So all's well that ends well.

So that draws a close to my tales of Burlington Road. I don't think I've forgotten anybody, have I? I'm joking of course. I know I haven't mentioned my main character, my little man Bogart.

Well Bogart, or Duke as he now answers to, (cats are so fickle) still has the run of Burlington Road and I'm told is still terrorised by the local robins. He has adopted Joaquin and his family now, and is as fat, pampered and happy as he ever was. I'm sure you'll be pleased to learn that. We are after all, a nation of animal lovers.

Just one more person to mention now, the real hero of this story. No, not me! Zachary, my childhood friend. I never saw him again after that night and neither has Joaquin, who surprised me by asking who the young lad was that he'd seen in my house. I do feel him around me sometimes, and it gives me comfort just knowing he's there and looking out for me.

Epilogue

The sun has dipped into the ocean bed, leaving only a thin, orange streak across the horizon. Soon the sea and the sky will merge into a vast, inky nothingness. A black velvet backdrop displaying a multitude of diamante stars.

Down in the bay, a solitary fishing boat bobbles about on a sea as calm as any millpond, and a string of harbour lights twinkle and dance on the wind's breath.

One by one the street vendors and artists pack away their goods and leave. The tourists drift away from the front, and the seafood and paella restaurants enjoy a brief lull before the evening masses descend.

The quayside is empty now, save for a lone pale-faced boy stood beneath the old iron street-lantern. He slowly turns his head and looks up at Jared's window and his smile is radiant in the glow of the lamp. He lingers a while longer, silently watching the patio curtain blowing in the cool evening breeze, before turning away and disappearing into the night.

Keep reading for an excerpt
from the newest book
by Jack C. Phillips

A Strange Encounter at Little Hubery

Coming soon from Camelot Press

Prologue

The man leant against the parapet and straightened his tie. The view from bridge three-sixty-one allowed him to see for miles around, but the woodland, coastline and untamed natural beauty of the surrounding moorland held no charm for him. Not today.

It had been another hot day and the sun was setting on the horizon, weaving braids of fiery red across the sky. The man wiped beads of perspiration from his forehead and looked at his fob-watch. Only another ten minutes to go and then it would all be over. He thought of his fiancée and how he'd let her down. He hoped that she'd understand and that one day she'd be able to forgive him.

Five minutes now and his mouth felt parched. His hands were shaking and his vision blurred. He thought he could hear the approaching engine, the York express, a 0-6-0 Saddle tank locomotive pulling four coaches. He heard the low whistle down the line and the faint humming of the vibrating track. He knew the engine was building up a good head of steam as it worked hard against the grade, and he heard the familiarly comforting rhythmical clunk of the side irons. He fancied he could smell the burning fuel, just whispers of smoke on the wind's breath. And then he saw her on the horizon, emerging from the tunnel like a beautiful armoured goddess of war. A testament to power and ingenuity, her paintwork gleaming in the bright sunlight. A vision of splendour shimmering and wavering in the incandescent heat.

Trembling now, he climbed over and onto the narrow ledge, the roar becoming deafening as the train approached.

'Please God, forgive me!' he cried out in anguish. He paused for a second as he thought he heard the sweetest of voices calling out his name, and he looked around him blindly, his eyes swimming with tears. The train was but a few feet away and he knew the voice was in his head, that he would never again hear his beloved Elizabeth.

But Elizabeth was calling him…Elizabeth was there. She'd arrived at the bridge just in time to see her husband-to-be throw himself off the ledge and into the path of the oncoming train.

A Strange Encounter at Little Hubery
By Jack C. Phillips

Seven strangers are trapped in a remote and lonely railway station on the desolate Yorkshire moors when a freak storm brings a tree down on the tracks. As railway staff battle to clear the line further north, it becomes apparent that those stranded will be there for the night, and they reluctantly settle down in the waiting room as the storm rages about the exposed moorland.

Who lurks in the dimly lit station, watching the passengers as they huddle around the fire? And what lies in wait for them outside on the storm-tossed moor? One by one, stories are told and secret revealed, and it soon becomes unnervingly evident to those seeking sanctuary at the old station that things at Little Hubery are not what they seem.

A real spine-tingler to curl up with beneath the duvet on a cold winter's night.

Printed in Germany
by Amazon Distribution
GmbH, Leipzig